BARON

SHANNON HEIGHTON HICKS

IRON BACK WARRIORS

BLIND LOVE
BARON

BARON

IRON BACK WARRIORS

SHANNON **HEIGHTON HICKS**

Baron

Copyright 2019 by Shannon Heighton Hicks

EDITOR: VIRGINIA TESI CAREY

DESIGN: RMGRAPHX

COVER MODEL: JOHNNY KANE

COVER PHOTOGRAPHER: ERIC DAVID BATTERSHELL

For Jon-Eric, one of the best dads I have ever known.

"A harmless man is not a good man. A good man is a very dangerous man who has that under voluntary control"
– Jordan Peterson

CHAPTER 1

"Murphy!" Baron barked into the phone. Two in the morning was not a time for a wrong number. Not recognizing the number, he wanted to tell the person to fuck off. His mind instantly went to his alarm clock that was scheduled to go off at 4:00 A.M.

As he glared at the clock, he heard a female voice ask, "Is this Baron Murphy? Sir?"

He snapped, "Who's asking?"

"This is Doris Smith with County Hospital in Bedford, Virginia. Are you Jade Murphy's husband?"

Baron sat straight up in bed and asked, "What about her?"

"Sir, are you Baron Murphy, Jade Murphy's husband?"

"Yeah, yeah! Is she there? Is she hurt?"

"Mr. Murphy, I'm not sure how to explain what has happened..."

"Just say it... Is she dead?"

"No, oh no! Not at all! She has given birth. You are listed as the father. She—"

"What did you say?" Baron yelled into the phone.

"Mr. Murphy, please let me continue."

The lady from the hospital went on to explain that Jade had delivered a full-term baby girl, as yet unnamed. From there she explained that Jade had given them his information as she had no one to come and get her and the baby and nowhere to go.

Baron responded with grunts and mm-hmms when asked if he understood. He told her he was leaving right away. After he hung up, he sat, stunned, for a few minutes. Getting up, he quickly packed a bag, not knowing how long he would be in Virginia. Stressed, he called his dad.

"King. Son? Everything okay?"

"Not really. Can I drop Nate off?"

He went on to explain the call he just received.

"Son of a bitch!" King roared.

"Dad, what am I going to do?"

"Go get your girl. Leave that bitch."

Baron sighed. "Dad, come on."

"Just drop him off, son. I'll call to see if someone can go with you."

"I think Romeo has the next forty-eight off."

"I'll call him first."

"Thanks, Dad."

Hanging up, Baron quietly woke up Nate. As his son trudged into the bathroom, Baron packed up some clothes for him.

"Dad, it's still dark out. Why did you get me up?" Nate grumbled.

"Sorry, little man. I have to go up to Virginia. I just got a call to go."

Nate looked at him. "Can I go with you?"

"I wish I could take you. Next time, okay?"

Nate looked at him seriously. "Is this about Mom?"

Baron paused. He owed him the truth, but what if it was all a lie?

Debating how much to tell him, he said, "Nate, I'm not sure

2

what is going on but I have to go see. Okay?"

Nate pressed his lips together, but they trembled anyway. "I don't want her to come back."

Baron pulled him by his shoulders and wrapped his arms around him.

"It will be all right. I am never leaving you again. I will always keep you safe. I promise." He hesitated, then added, "This is the only way to be sure."

Nate snuffled and nodded. Getting a tissue, he blew his nose.

Baron grabbed his bag, then stopped.

"You think you can learn how to bake something with Claire while I'm gone?"

Nate cocked his head and with eyebrows raised, said, "Oh. Challenge accepted!"

Baron laughed. "As if you need a reason to go see her, right?"

"As if," Nate replied, using one of Claire's favorite phrases.

Baron stuffed their bags in the back of the truck.

Shit, he thought. *I'm going to need a car seat and kinds of shit we haven't needed for years. Bedford, Virginia, should have a Target or Walmart, right?*

CHAPTER 2

Baron and Romeo made it to the hospital in Bedford, Virginia. They checked in at the visitor's desk for directions to the maternity floor. After a short elevator lift to the second floor, they stopped at the nurse's station. The nurse on duty looked up and blinked, then blushed at the two tall good-looking men in front of her. Romeo smiled and reached across the counter, taking her hand.

"Hello. I'm Andrew, a fellow nurse from Myrtle Beach. You ever make it down that way?"

Baron elbowed him out of the way. "Asshole," he grumbled at him.

Looking at the nurse, he stated, "I'm Baron Murphy. My wife, Jade, gave birth recently."

The nurse visibly blanched. "Oh, um, Mr. Murphy. Yes. Um, er…can you follow me, please?"

Nodding, he followed her to a small family counseling office. Baron was getting a bad feeling. He looked at Romeo who had an equally worried look on his face.

The nurse left and came back shortly with a social worker.

"Mr. Murphy? I'm Sandy Hamilton, a social worker with the

hospital," she introduced herself, shaking Baron's hand. "We are so glad you are here," she began.

"Well, you guys called me. Of course I came as soon as I could."

"Yes. Well, some things have changed since early this morning."

"What the hell does that mean? Is my baby okay?"

"Mr. Murphy, it seems, well…Mrs. Murphy left the premises sometime last night. We aren't sure when. She, she left the baby here."

Baron never realized he had sat down.

"Brother," Romeo said with his hand on his shoulder. "We can get through this. The baby is still here. Right?" he asked the social worker.

"How could she just leave? Again? I thought I had finally found her. Could get some fucking answers, more for Nate than me. She left him. How could she leave the baby with no one? She at least knew Nate had my mom or dad. What the fuck was she thinking?" he roared.

A nurse rushed in and asked him to keep it down.

Romeo stood up. "Get out. I got this."

The nurse shot him a look but left and closed the door with the social worker following her.

"Baron, you have got to keep your cool through all of this. You are all that baby girl has right now. She has you. You got this. And WE have your back. Always." He bumped fists with Baron. "Now. We need to be prepared for any legal shit there may be."

"Like what?" Baron asked.

"Don't know, man. You were contacted so obviously she listed you. You've got ID. Just…man…I know how she was when you were gone. Are you sure? Could it be…?"

"The timing's right. It matches up from when I was last home," Baron replied, deep in thought. "Either way, she is mine now. No one else is raising Nate's sister but me. She is coming home with us. Period."

Romeo nodded. "Fair enough."

Baron spent the rest of the day signing forms and consent. When it came to the labor and delivery charges and the hospital bills, he just shook his head. "We have insurance. Just bill me for whatever we owe after that."

Just as he was coming to the end of his patience, there was another knock at the door.

"Knock, knock. Daddy? Are you ready to see your little girl?"

Baron was standing instantly, reaching for his little girl.

"I imagine you have done this before? I know she has a big brother at home from what your wife said," the last part she said quietly.

Baron nodded. His eyes were on the bundle in the basinet. All he could see was a pink cap and swaddled blanket. *What did she look like? Was she fair like her mom? Did she have dark hair?* His baby girl he just found out about. He wanted to hold her like he needed his last breath.

The nurse picked her up. "It's about time for her to eat again, if you want to feed her?"

He nodded as she placed the bundle in his arms. Laughing softly, he wiped a tear on his shoulder. She looked at him as he looked at her. Her eyes were gray like his. He said the first thing that came to him, "I love you, baby girl," his voice, husky with emotion.

"Oh man, she is beautiful, Baron," Romeo murmured, smiling at the baby as he looked over Baron's shoulder.

"She is. More than anything," Baron murmured back.

The nurse smiled at the three, and asked, "What will you call her? Have you had a chance to think of that?"

Baron looked up, brow furrowed. "What did she name her?"

The nurse paused before walking out. "She didn't. That will

be up to you, Daddy."

Instead of giving into the anger he felt, he looked at his daughter. "That I can do," he whispered to her.

CHAPTER 3

After Baron and Romeo took enough pictures and sent them to everyone, King called him.

"I make some beautiful grandkids!" he laughed.

Baron chuffed. "Sure, I didn't have something to do with her beauty and Nate's old man?"

"Old man my arse! When are you bringing our girl home?"

"I have to GET her home first. She has to stay another day, then she can go. I'm not leaving her. Romeo is going to go shopping."

"I am? Christ! I have no idea what to get!" Romeo could be heard yelling in the background.

"Claire will email you both a list of what you will need to get her home. By the way, when will our princess have a name?"

Baron grinned. "Princess? Her name is Amanda. After Baronne's old lady. She would have loved her."

"Shit, son. That's perfect. Thank you."

"All right, before I get all misty again. I got the list. She should sleep most, if not all, the way back, don't you think?"

"Should I guess?"

"Can you guys pick up a portable crib or something until I

can make it to the store at home?"

Baron could hear the door to King's house open and close. "We'll get you through, son. Don't worry.

***

Romeo came through. He had found a Walmart and had smooth talked a female customer into helping him find the items on the list Claire had sent them. He came back with wipes, diapers, cloth diapers (why they needed both he had no clue), bottles, some "pink" newborn outfits, socks, blankets, and an infant car seat (reverse facing, he had at least known that). He also threw in snacks and water for the ride home. Knowing Baron, there would be no stopping if he could help it. Romeo couldn't blame him. At the last minute, Romeo threw aspirin and beer into the cart. He had a headache and would drink the beer at the hotel that night. He needed it.

The car seat manual had each of them hanging out one side or the other of the SUV.

"It doesn't make any sense!" Baron fumed, scratching his head. "Why is it not tight enough? What are these other straps for?"

"What the hell is an anchor?" Romeo asked, equally puzzled.

They both stood, hands on hips with murderous looks on their faces. People had stopped walking to look and stare. Baron shot them a withering look and they moved on, though reluctantly.

"Let me see the instructions again." Baron motioned for the paper booklet.

Romeo handed it over and opened a water. "Did I pick out the most difficult seat or are they all like this?"

"They are like this to be safe. I'm sure that is why it is hard to get them in. Though that doesn't make sense when you think about it," Baron replied, reading the booklet. "Well fuck me. The damn anchors are between the seat back and the seat bottom. That is what the extra straps are for." Reaching between the seat back and bottom, he found a metal piece to attach the hook to. Pulling the straps tighter, the base was finally in snug and secure.

"I need a drink," Baron grumbled.

Shaking his head at that idea, he began going through the clothes, blankets, and socks Romeo had purchased and already washed in natural detergent (again, per Claire's instruction). Baron picked out two outfits for her to have pictures in and to go home in. After this they were both exhausted. They both took some aspirin and a coffee then went back into the hospital to get Amanda.

As Romeo gave Amanda a bottle for the road (he was pretty pleased with himself on that one), Baron signed release forms and care sheets for Amanda, confirming he did indeed have some clue as to how to take care of a baby.

They thanked everyone and left the hospital. Placing Amanda's car seat in the base that was hooked into the car. They both individually checked twice to make sure that it was secure. The hospital had given them enough formula for the ride home. On the way out of Bedford, Romeo pulled into the Welcome Center for the town. He ran in and came back out with a bag.

At Baron's questioning look, he replied, "For Nate. It's just a shirt with the D-Day Memorial on it," he said. "Kinda cool. Couldn't not pick up something for my godson."

Baron smiled. "Thanks, man. Shit. I didn't even know that was here. Claire is the history buff. Guess I will have to ask her about the places in Virginia besides Arlington, you know?"

Rome nodded. "Sure enough. Let's roll. I need my bed and this princess needs to meet her big brother!"

CHAPTER 4

They made it back home after only a couple of stops to change and feed her. Pulling into Baron's driveway, they noticed that the street, yard, and half of the driveway were packed with friends and family. Baron and Romeo both grinned as Nate came barreling out the door, running to Baron's side of the SUV. "Dad! You're home!" he shouted, launching himself at Baron. Baron laughed and hugged him tight.

"Is that my sister?" Nate whispered, loudly. Baron looked at him.

***

"What do you think about that?"

"I'd like to see her."

Baron nodded and they walked around to the other side of the SUV.

"This beach sun is too strong for her right now. Let's get her inside where you can meet her."

Baron took the seat out of the car. Other club members were

already getting the bags out of the back of the SUV. *It's good to be home.* As he walked up to the house, he saw all of the pink balloons he had missed at the mailbox. People patted him on the back and cooed and complimented the baby.

Making his way inside, he saw his Dad, leaned against the doorway, a beer in hand.

Motioning to follow him, King said, "Come on to her room."

Baron, Nate, and Amanda followed him. Baron was blown away. The room was beautiful. It was pink and gold. There was a round baby bed with pink netting around it. There was a cream colored dresser, changing table, and glider rocker. The closet, dresser, and changing table were full of wipes, diapers, clothes, bibs, blankets, and more.

Nate sat in the rocker. "I'm ready to hold her now."

Baron cleared his throat a few times. "It's too much, Dad. Y'all shouldn't have."

"Well, your Mom and Claire kind of took over and then put us all to work. It was worth it, son. One last thing for you to not have to worry about," King responded.

Baron looked at Nate. "You sure you are ready?"

Nate grinned. "No better time to start than right now. Right?" *This kid. My pride and joy. So proud of him.*

Baron kneeled in front of Nate and took Amanda out of her car seat. She stretched the stretch babies do without a care. As Nate held his arms out, Baron carefully placed her there, arranging Nate's arms around her.

"Hold her head up," Baron told him quietly.

Nate looked down at her. "You are kind of pretty for a baby," he told her. "You are my Manda. My Manda Panda."

Everyone laughed. Amanda looked at him seriously.

King laughed and said, "That's how these things begin. Nicknames and all."

Baron nodded and took Manda back from Nate. "Let's get

you changed, darling."

Nate went to the dresser and picked out a simple onesie with a ruffle on the bottom.

"She was a little sweaty," he told Baron as he handed him the outfit.

Baron laughed. "Well, let's take care of that then."

After she was changed, Baron turned to King. "Dad?"

"Your mom will kill me, but her loss and all!" King replied with a huge grin.

King took Manda carefully. He looked down at her and her eyes widened when she felt his soft beard.

***

"Hello, little one," his deep voice softened only for her. "You are the princess this club has waited for. You are perfect."

King made his way to the living room and sat beside Priest who nodded.

"Aye brother, she'll do," he said, grinning and winking at his niece.

"That will do, Priest. Between you and Romeo, the baby will know nothing but scoundrels!" Sasha, king's ex-wife said, taking Manda in her arms. "You'll be a good girl. No biker scoundrels for you."

"Oi, away with you, you old nag. Who asked you anyway?" Priest asked, showing his teeth.

Claire sat beside him and said, "You will always be my scoundrel," as she put her hand against his cheek.

King watched as Priest leaned into her hand, shutting his eyes.

"Always for you my love and you," he murmured to Ranger who sat across from him.

"Rawr," he said after her, making claws with his hands, causing them all to laugh quietly.

"You all are bad," snickered Dani as she came in the room carrying Manda.

"What's this? How did you get her?" accused Claire good-naturedly.

Claire carefully took Manda from Dani and sat down again beside Priest.

"That was quite the maneuver there yourself, Trouble," Priest said with a grin.

Ranger sat down on the other side of Claire and felt two sets of eyes on him.

"Are you sure?" Claire whispered.

Ranger looked at her confused. "About?"

"You don't want any more?"

"Yes. I have never been more sure about anything except my love for both of you."

Claire looked down at Manda and smiled.

Nate came over and sat on the coffee table in front of them.

"Aunt Claire, Dad doesn't believe me when I said I made the cupcakes and Uncle Romeo said they taste store bought!"

From the kitchen, they could hear whistles and an "oh shit!", then a door to outside opening and closing. Someone yelled, "Run, Romeo, Run!"

"Oh no he didn't!" responded Claire. Turning, she gently placed Manda in Priest's arms and went after Romeo.

"Wait! What? Woman, what have you done?" yelled Priest which in turn made Manda cry. "Christ! What now?" Priest asked, looking at Ranger.

Snorting, Ranger held out his hands. "Give her to me."

Taking her from Priest, Ranger stood and walked back to her room with Baron following. Ranger changed her diaper and sat down in the rocker with her, taking the bottle from Baron. Baron stood there, stunned.

"Just helping out. This help won't be here forever," Ranger

murmured, looking at Manda.

"But how did…" Baron began.

Ranger smiled a soft smile and said, "I have a daughter. She is in fact about to make me a granddad."

Baron leaned against the door looking at him. He realized that though the man was a brother, loved his uncle and Claire, there had been very little time for him to get to know him.

"Granddad, huh? My old man knows that feeling two times over now."

"Yeah. I'm really looking forward to it. I just wish she were closer is all. Moments like this again. Love it. I also love the fact that these small moments are not my life. I've grown to love being an adult who worries about the other two adults in my life. Not about sleepovers, little league and all that. My job just doesn't work either. Homicide is 24/7. No schedule involved at times."

Ranger raised Manda to his shoulder and burped her. "She's a good baby. She's also out for the count. Do you want me to lay her in her crib? I swear the sheets and blanket have been washed to General Claire's specifications!"

Baron chuffed and said, "She takes that stuff seriously, right?"

Ranger nodded and laid Manda in her crib, placing her blanket over her. They one armed hugged, shaking hands which caused Claire to snort as she had been quietly watching them.

"General Claire?" she asked.

"Yes General. Only to your liking," Ranger responded and pulled her to him.

"Okay. Yep. Out. Getting uncomfortable," Baron grumbled, walking down the hallway.

***

Big Easy made his way outside and handed a beer to Baron. Baron drank half of it down then set the bottle aside. He kept the baby monitor close by but picked it up anyway.

Bigs lay his hand on his shoulder. "Take all the time you need, brother."

"You know I can't do that, man. I only just got back. I have another mouth to feed now."

"You're covered."

"Screw that. I pull my weight."

"I know. Your family needs you now."

Baron hissed a breath between his teeth, shaking his head. "Two weeks."

"Four. Final offer." Bigs stuck his hand out and Baron shook it.

"Thanks, man."

"Take care of the kids. Get Nate back in school. We'll talk some more then."

Sasha came out and wrapped her arms around Baron's neck. "There's cake and presents waiting."

"Momma! You guys have done so much already…too much!"

"Swallow that pride, son of mine. This was all done in love. From the club."

***

After more bath stuff and clothes, strollers, another car seat, books and stuff Baron really wasn't sure what it was, *google that later*, Baron wished everyone a good night.

Manda made her farewell known by squealing into the baby monitor. Sasha went in to change her so Baron could prepare her bottle.

"She has such a tiny butt," she said, patting Manda's butt.

"It can stay that way too," Baron replied, taking Manda from his mom.

Nate was finishing off a second piece of cake. *Thank goodness no school tomorrow,* Baron thought to himself.

"Hey, bud, prospects will come by tomorrow to clean up. Throw your stuff away and hit the shower," Baron told Nate. "Brush your teeth real good."

CHAPTER 5

Baron slowly rocked Manda Panda, grinning at the nickname. His grin softened as he looked down at her. Her chin was tucked to her shoulder, her soft hair forming ringlets. He stroked her tiny hand with his finger.

The active day was finally hitting him. Yawning, he stood up, walked to the crib and gently lay her down, covering her with a blanket. Stroking her head, he smiled when she let out a big sigh and slept on. Walking out of the room, he pulled the door almost shut. He walked to Nate's room and watched his son looking through his books. Nate's collection had grown since his tutoring sessions with Claire had gone so well. He was now in the top reading level of his class. He would be moving to the fourth grade in the fall.

"What are you reading to me tonight?" he asked Nate.

Nate pondered his choices and asked, "Can I start reading to Manda now too?"

Baron was touched by his son's kindness. "Of course you can," he replied. "I'm sure she will love that."

Nate nodded and grinned, still pondering the books in

front of him. "You know, she will need her own books. I should probably read books she will understand."

Baron smiled tiredly. "I think that is a good plan. Right now, I think hearing your voice is all she needs. You are going to be a great big brother. I'm kinda jealous. I never had a brother like you."

Nate looked at him. "Why?"

Baron shrugged. "I guess I was more than enough for gramma and grampa."

Nate seesawed his head side to side. "Maybe."

Nate chose a book and Baron sat beside him as he read it.

"You read so well," he told Nate.

"I really like it," Nate replied.

"Mind if I tuck you in? I think I am going to sleep a little before Manda is up for her bottle."

Nate nodded and climbed under the covers. Baron tucked him in and gave him a kiss on top of the head.

"Night, killa," he said to Nate.

"Night, Daddy," Nate replied with a yawn.

***

Manda Panda woke up twice during the night. She needed her diaper changed and her bottle then went happily back to sleep. *Ranger was right, she is a good baby.*

As Baron sipped some coffee and rubbed his eyes, Pretty came in the back door.

"Hey brother," Pretty said, offering an arm grip.

"Hey, man. Thanks for coming. Who else is coming to help?" Baron asked, looking at Manda, who was in her car seat. Reaching over he gently rocked it. Manda looked at him and he smiled back at her.

"Otter and Cowboy were just pulling in when I got here."

"Cool. If we can get things cleaned up, I could use some help getting some of her stuff put together. Especially the countertop swing and the standing swing. I plan on having a place for her no matter where we are in the house."

"Bet. Anything you need," Pretty replied.

"I'll order lunch for us later," Baron said as the other two prospects came in the door.

"Brother," Cowboy said as he stopped to look at Manda. "She is a beauty."

"Thanks. I have to say I agree." Baron grinned.

"Can I hold her?" Otter asked shyly.

"Sure," Baron replied, picking her up. "You know how, right?" he asked, pausing before handing her over.

"Yeah, I have younger siblings back home," Otter replied, as Baron gently placed her in his arms.

"Hey there pretty girl," Otter whispered, slowly rocking back and forth with her.

She looked at him and sneezed.

Laughing, he said, "Nothing to sneeze at, darling. You are too cute."

Nate came in the kitchen. "Dad, I'm hungry. Do we have breakfast?" he asked, eyeing the cake.

"We do. Not cake. What do you want?"

"Just cereal. I'll get it. I'm going fishing off the dock in a little bit."

"Okay. You know to be careful right? Anyone else going?"

"Uncle Priest and Ranger are going with me."

Baron nodded, glad his uncle and Ranger were taking time to hang out with Nate. As he was taking Manda back from Otter, his dad came into the kitchen.

"There's my girl and boy," King said, looking at Nate.

"Grampa!" Nate yelled, running over and hugging King. "I want to go fishing in a little while. Do you want to come?"

"I plan to a little later. I am spending time with both of my grandkids today."

"Ok. We won't catch all of the fish before you come out there."

King smiled at him and ruffled his hair. "You better not. It's already hot out there. Go get your sunscreen so we can put it on."

Baron sat and took a big breath, letting it in and out. Manda was asleep in her baby seat. Looking over at King, he waited for the questions. He didn't have to wait long.

"She just left her there?" King asked quietly, looking at Manda.

"Seems so. The nurses said that she was just gone when they came in to check on her." Baron paused. "How could she do this to both kids? Why are we not enough? I just don't get it. I know I was gone a lot but she never told me she was unhappy. I guess I should have clued into it somehow. Nate doesn't want her to come back. He seemed really upset at the thought that she would come back."

"She really wasn't a mother when she had Nate. We stepped in where we could. It was hard to know how far we should step in out of respect for your marriage. I wish to hell we had now. I feel like I let you and Nate down. I'm sorry about that, son. She wasn't mother material at 15. That's why you two don't have a third child with you now. If her parents hadn't taken the child, who knows how things would be for that girl now," King said quietly. It was obvious how much all of it bothered him. The guilt was obvious.

Baron put his hand on his dad's arm. "You have the responsibility of so many on you. I don't blame you for anything. I want you to know that. We all have our own shit to deal with. Nate and Manda are safe now. That is what matters. If anything, it has made Nate very self-sufficient. I'm grateful for that at least. If he weren't, I have a feeling having Manda would be an even greater challenge. So far, she seems to be a good baby. I didn't have the whole baby experience of much of any experience with Nate. I regret it but at the same time, I'm glad for it. It enabled me to gain skills and invest in the business with Bigs.

King bowed his head in thought. Looking up, he gazed at Manda and then Baron. Smiling, he said, "We have a princess. Can you believe it? This family of men. After all of this time?"

Baron chuckled. "I can't. It is just mind-blowing. Of course it has only been a few days. We didn't exactly get the nine month build up like most people do. I'm going to do better for her than I did Nate. Her and Nate. They are going to be my focus. No one else comes before them. Ever. I am a dad and dad only."

King cocked an eyebrow at him. "You say that now but there will be someone else for you. Someone that will be perfect for this family. Don't give up on that, Baron."

Baron had no response. He really wasn't in the mindset for anything else.

CHAPTER 6

Things were not going well. Baron loved his kids to death but could not work from home when they were there. Manda was staying awake longer through the day and sleeping longer through the night. That was great when she slept, but some things had to be handled at night. Running a security company could be a twenty-four hour a day job.

Baron was pondering what to do as he took Manda out of her little tub. He wrapped her up in a towel and hugged her close. She always smelled so good after her bath. As he sifted through a drawer for her jammies his stomach felt wet suddenly. He looked at her.

"You did it again didn't you?" She looked back and smiled.

"Why do you keep peeing on your old man? It's not very ladylike."

Sighing, he laid her on the changing table. Pulling out some wipes, he wiped down her legs. When he was finished, she happily grabbed her toes. He cocked an eyebrow at her and finished cleaning her. After her diaper, Baron put her in her soft giraffe pajamas. She loved having prints or something special on her feet. He sometimes found her singing or talking to her feet in the morning when she woke up.

As he sat in the rocker with her, he pondered his options. He had room for a live-in nanny. Could he handle some stranger living in the house with them? How did you handle personal space? Would he want them to handle cleaning as well? That in itself had been a challenge. The three of them could make the house a mess. Fast. He had tried to keep up with it all, but with work, club, and Nate's extra activities besides his school, it was challenging. Baron had set up stations though out the house for Manda so he could work, cook, or do things with Nate. He had tried to stay away from delivery for their meals, although it had been very tempting. Eating healthy for all of them was important to Baron.

What if he wanted to go out with someone? He wouldn't bring them home. That was out of the question. Then again he hadn't had the opportunity in months. He was just too busy and if he were honest with himself, there just had been no interest. Typically, he was too tired anyway. Christ, he was in his twenties. Not dead. With a big sigh, he rubbed his eyes. Looking down, he saw that Manda was asleep.   Placing her in the crib, he looked down at her. His chest hurt from how much he loved her. He could have stood there and watched her sleep all night, but he needed sleep. Picking up her bottle, he headed to the kitchen. He rinsed the bottle and put it in the dishwasher with their dishes from dinner. Leaning against the counter, he listened to the dishwasher as it ran and put his head in his hands, rubbing up and down his face. He needed help.

Christmas had come and gone. He felt good about how the house had been decorated and felt it had been a great first Christmas for Manda. Not that she would remember it anyway, but he and Nate would. His mom had pretty much been scarce since then. That was no surprise. He knew Claire would help but she was still recovering from her kidnapping and subsequent illness. Gritting his teeth, Baron thought about Anderson. Shaking his head of that thought, he walked to Nate's room.

Nate was out cold. Walking over, Baron pulled the covers over him, pulled the book out of his hands and placed it on the shelf. Picking up the clothes and towel off the floor he walked out of the room and headed to the laundry room to put them in the washing machine. The laundry was piling up. *Shit,* he thought. Maybe household chores would be part of the nanny's duties. Yawning so big his jaw cracked, he headed to bed.

Baron was on his face, asleep. In the back of his mind something said he was not alone. Snapping awake, he reached for his gun, that was not there. Looking, he saw it was Nate. Blinking, he looked at the clock. Seven A.M. *What the hell?* Sitting up, he took Manda from Nate.

"How long have you guys been up?" he asked Nate, still not quite awake.

"Not long. I was heading to the kitchen when I heard her. Manda Panda was talking to her feet," Nate said, tickling her feet. She giggled and kicked her feet. "I didn't change her because, you know, that's gross."

Baron huffed a laugh. "Thanks for getting her, bud. And thank you Manda Panda for sleeping in a little." After he said that, Baron frowned. Then realization hit him. "You slept through the night! What a champ!" he said, kissing her on top of her head.

Nate took her little hand and gave her a high five.

"Nah!" she said in reply.

Baron and Nate both laughed at this.

"Can you stay with her, here on the bed while I am in the bathroom?" Baron asked Nate.

"Yeah, Dad. I got it." Nate lay beside her on the bed, pretending to bite her feet. Baron ran into the bathroom hearing her deep giggles.

After Baron had washed his hands, he came back out and scooped her up.

"Thanks again, Nate. You are a big help and a great big brother!"

"Thanks, Dad. I love her. She's my baby too," Nate replied to his Dad, walking out of the room.

Baron took Manda to her room and lay her on the changing table. After taking off her pajamas and changing her diaper, he took her to the closet.

"What are you wearing today little Miss? A dress? Leggings? You are such a diva already," he teased her, with a grin. Stopping he realized he knew way too much about girl's clothes, way too soon. Shaking his head and rolling his eyes, he got her dressed.

Once Manda was dressed, Baron brought her into the kitchen and set her in her baby seat. He noticed that Nate was cutting up a banana in his cereal.

Nate looked up at him. "What?"

Baron grinned. "Never seen you do that is all."

Nate shrugged. "You and Aunt Claire want me to eat healthier. I like it too, so why not?"

"I'm glad you like it. Are you packing or buying lunch today?"

"Packing," Nate said, making a face. "It's tomato soup day. Disgusting."

Baron snorted. "Okay, but you know, you eat Claire's tomato soup."

"Yeah. Claire's is different. She adds that leaf stuff. It's good. What is it again?"

"Basil?"

"Yeah. And I can add cheese and crackers and stuff. Her grilled cheese is amazing too."

Baron couldn't argue with that. Manda was at the end of her patience, though, and began to cry. Baron looked at her and began making her cereal, feeling bad he had waited too long.

Sitting down he spooned some cereal into her mouth. She began opening her mouth like a baby bird, waiting for the next precious spoonful. She was no diva when it came to eating. Eating was serious business. After the last spoonful had been eaten, Baron wiped her face with a soft cloth, causing her to laugh.

While Nate went to get dressed and to brush his teeth, Baron packed Nate's lunch under Manda's watchful eye. Picking up different items for her approval, Baron kept her occupied and happy, laughing at her reactions. The raise of a delicate eyebrow usually meant no or yes. He went with it either way, grinning at her. Baron also took time to pack her bag with bottles, formula, diapers, wipes, clothes, blankets, and bibs. He debated packing more toys, but knew there was more at the office.

Nate came bounding into the kitchen, grabbing his backpack and lunchbox and rushed out the door. Baron waited and looked up when Nate came back in the house.

"I'm putting my stuff into the truck!" Nate yelled and ran back outside.

"Okay, going to get dressed and I will be there," Baron said to the air.

Placing Manda in the center of the bed in her seat, Baron quickly got dressed and brushed his teeth. It always made him nervous to leave her alone, even though he knew she was perfectly safe buckled into her seat. Walking back into the room, he saw her looking up at the ceiling, blowing bubbles out of her mouth. He looked up at the ceiling fan and back at her.

"It's pretty cool, huh?" he asked her.

Not expecting a response, he picked her up, grabbing her bag. He stopped only to gently put her in her car seat, tucking a blanket around her for warmth. Pausing, he kissed her on her forehead. She grinned a toothless grin at him that made his day.

CHAPTER 7

After dropping Nate off at school, Baron and Manda headed to his office. Pulling into his parking spot, Baron looked back at Manda. As he figured, she was fast asleep. Grabbing her bag, he carefully unhooked her seat from the base. Carrying her in, he quickly made his way to his office, placing her gently in the pack and play he had set up for her. Sitting down at his desk, he took a deep breath. He had not eaten or had any coffee that morning. Reaching into the mini fridge he kept in his office, he popped the top off a bottle of water and guzzled it down. Walking out of his office, he headed to the break room needing coffee. Rolling his head on his shoulders, he popped a pod in the coffee maker and waited. He inhaled the fragrant brew, lost in thought. He drank his coffee black. The first sip was bliss.

Walking back into his office, he perused the files that had been left on his desk. With his stomach growling, he called in an order for breakfast for everyone. Sometime later, there was a knock at his door. He looked up as the door opened and groaned inwardly, as Tabby came in with a plate.

"Tabby, what are you doing here?" Tabby had given up on

winning his uncle over and had set her sights on him, or so he had been told.

"I work in the coffee shop now. Claire put in a good word for me. I made a plate for you so you wouldn't have to stop working."

"She did? Oh. Um, thanks," he mumbled, accepting the plate.

He glanced over warily, as Tabby walked over to see Manda. She cooed at her but didn't wake her up.

"She is such a doll, Baron," she said softly. "If you ever need someone to watch her, my roommate is great with kids. She just moved here."

"I'll keep that in mind," he said around a mouthful of food.

"Well, I need to get going back to the coffee shop. Have a great day, Baron."

"You too, Tabby."

"Oh. Hey, I go by Tabitha now. It sounds more professional."

Baron was speechless. *Tabitha, not Tabby,* he thought, as she gave a little wave and left.

***

As he finished eating, Baron got a call from Bigs, asking him to head to the conference room. Manda Panda woke up as he was gathering items to take. Quickly, he changed her, got her bottle ready, stuffed his phone in his pocket, his tablet under his arm, and then picked her up to head out the door. As he balanced her bottle under his chin while feeding her, he opened and closed the door and made his way to the conference room. He entered the conference room and tossed everything on the table except for Manda and the bottle. Bigs grinned at his longtime friend.

"There's my girl. She brought an adorable baby with her, too, I see," Bigs said, looking at Manda and Baron.

"Fuck you," Baron growled at Bigs, then winced looking

back down at Manda.

"Language big daddy, language," Bigs teased. "Though hanging around this crew, she will pick up a word or two for sure. Who knows what else she will pick up?"

Baron's brow creased with worry and Manda let out a large burp looking over Baron's shoulder.

"My point exactly, young lady. Good job!" Bigs grinned at her.

"Geez, dude. No. I have to make a decision about this soon. I can't keep bringing her here and I can rarely get anything done at home."

"I know what you are saying, brother. Right now is fine. We love having her here, but when she starts moving around, she could get hurt," Bigs replied in sympathy.

"It's not just here though. Nate is getting involved in more activities which is great, don't get me wrong. I want him to do his stuff but I also want to be there to see him do it. I missed so much of his life when I was overseas. Now with…." He stopped but his face grew dark with the unsaid.

"Don't even say it, man. She chose to leave. Your kids are better off," Bigs said firmly.

Baron nodded, though it was clear his thoughts were elsewhere. Manda made a snorting noise. He picked her up to burp her again. She smiled, looking at Bigs and rubbed her face in Baron's shirt. A big, wet burp came out of her, causing Baron to look down at his shirt. *Well shit.*

"Shirt number two for me. Bath number one for her," he told Bigs.

"In other words, Manda Panda, two. Daddy, zero," Bigs said, laughing at Baron.

Baron gave him a dirty look. "This is going to be you, one day. You just wait."

"No way, man. I am too careful for that to happen. I am okay with it never happening, truth be told. I am not father material."

Baron looked at his friend and began to comment, when the rest of the team came in. He sat through the meeting, but after a while, the smell became too much. He got up with Manda and gathered their things.

"I'll put you guys on when we get in my truck. I need to get her home and in the bath. We both need it," he said, grimacing.

He felt bad about pausing the meeting and making them wait, but he had to do right by Manda. On the way to his house, he made occasional input to the meeting, but his last thought stayed with him. Was he really doing right by her by taking her to the office? She should be home in a nurturing environment. Baron knew she was given love and care while she was with him at the office, but his time was always divided. She needed fresh air, activity, and…his thoughts paused…a mom. Thunking his head against the headrest of his seat, he pushed that thought out of his mind.

Hopping out of the truck, he opened the back door and got her out. He was surprised that she was still awake, but since she still needed a bath, he was happy to see that she was awake. Taking her straight to the bathroom, he ran the water till it was the right temperature and set her tub to filling. Undressing her, his thoughts were still filled with decisions he had to make. Placing her in the tub, he gently washed her hair and bathed her. He rubbed her tiny feet with a soft cloth which made her giggle. Soon though, her attention was on the toy that hung on the side of the tub. She loved to watch the bubbles that came out of it and watch the lights. While she was occupied, Baron took off his shirt and leaned back against the cabinet. Idly, he watched her and inwardly sighed again. Leaning over he took her out of the tub and wrapped her in her hooded towel, pausing, he gathered another thicker towel for security.

The light filtered in through her curtains casting a soft glow as he put a fresh diaper and onesie on her. Sitting in the rocker, he gently rocked back and forth with her, his mind still working out details and trying to come up with a solution. After some time, he looked down at her. She was asleep. Gently, he lay her in her crib, placing a blanket over here. Grabbing the baby monitor, he headed to his room for a shower.

Shucking his clothes, he turned the water in the shower to hot. Standing under the spray of water, he braced his hands against the wall of the shower and let the water run over his neck and shoulders. Slowly, he began washing his hair and body. He felt like he was asleep only not. After drying himself off, he pulled on some shorts and crawled into bed, falling asleep immediately.

CHAPTER 8

Cassidy Greene needed a job. What little savings she had was going toward rent, utilities, and what little food she had purchased when she has moved in with Tabitha. She was grateful that her childhood friend had allowed her to move in with her when she had needed a place to stay. It had been chance that she had seen her friend's post about needing a roommate. Cassidy had messaged her immediately. Now that she was here, she felt the oppressing dread she had felt in her last home lifting. The apartment was in a clean and simple complex close to the beach. Everything was in walking distance except for this "club" Tabitha was always talking about. Cassidy had not been to it. Clubbing wasn't her scene. Besides, she was getting ready to sell her car if she didn't find a job soon.

Cassidy was making a pitcher of lemonade when Tabitha came home. "Hey," they both said at the same time, making them both laugh.

"That looks like it will hit the spot," Tabitha said as she looked in the cabinet. "With a little of this," she added, holding a bottle of raspberry rum.

Cassidy frowned. "Lemonade and rum?"

"Watch and learn, little one," Tabitha said as she rimmed glasses with the rum and a little bit of sugar. She poured the rum and lemonade into the glasses with ice and stirred. She handed a glass to Cassidy. "Enjoy," she said, tapping her glass against Cassidy's.

Cassidy smiled and sipped her drink. "Oh yum!" she said, licking the sugar from her lips.

After Tabitha had changed out of her work clothes, they walked out onto their balcony to sit. They sipped their drinks and watched the waves.

This is paradise, Cassidy thought to herself. Compared to the oppression she had left, it was a miracle in her eyes.

"Hey, one of the guys from the club might need a babysitter or nanny for his baby and young son," Tabitha said, looking over her glass at Cassidy.

Cassidy thought about it. This might be what she was looking for. "Has he put up an ad or interviewed anyone?"

"Not that I know of," Tabitha responded.

Cassidy wondered about the type of services that would be needed and the pay. The drink was making her sleepy. Her phone buzzed. Looking at the screen, she sat up straight.

"I found you. You will return to me."

She broke into a cold sweat. She had been so careful. How had he found her? Getting up, she walked into the kitchen and washed out her glass. Tabitha followed her, concerned for her friend.

"Are you okay? You got that text and went white as a sheet. It's him, isn't it?"

Cass nodded. She was glad she had confided in Tabitha about leaving her last employer. That was the way she had been able to keep her name off the lease. Cassidy had gotten rid of her old phone and picked up a burner phone. Looking down at the message, she guessed she would have to get another phone now.

"What do you think he will do?" Tabitha asked, putting her hand on Cassidy's arm.

Cassidy shook her head. "I'm going to toss this phone and get a new one."

"You really need to get hired on with the club in some way. Let me see what they have going on. They will protect you."

"I don't think I need 'protection'," Cassidy mumbled. "I just want it to be over."

"Have you contacted an attorney?" Tabitha asked her.

"I don't have the money for one. There is a restraining order for what good that is doing."

"I'm really sorry this is happening," Tabitha gave her a hug.

"Me too," Cassidy sighed. "I was so happy there. Then it all went to hell so fast."

"Tomorrow. Tomorrow we start to get you on the right path."

"Yeah. I am going to bed," Cassidy said, sounding dejected.

Cassidy changed into an oversized t-shirt and climbed in bed. She was too preoccupied to wash her face. She just wanted to pull the blankets over her head, wanting to be away from the world, if only for a bit.

CHAPTER 9

King sat at the head of the table. Priest was to his left and Baron to his right. Romeo, Reaper, Viper, Bigs, Ranger, Vicious, and Ole Red sat at the rest of the seats at the table. On the agenda was filling employment positions at the campground and the bar. If possible, they were going to fill the receptionist spot at the tattoo parlor. Tiffany's death had been a huge hit to the club. They had paid for the funeral. The family was distraught and rightfully confused as to how this could have happened to their daughter. King's mind briefly went to Anderson. He closed his eyes against the fury that took over at the thought of Anderson. The man had kidnapped and tortured Claire, Priest and Ranger's woman, and then killed Tiffany. The police found no evidence to this conclusion, but the club knew. Anderson was not finished. Gritting his teeth against the thoughts of Anderson, King cracked his neck and began the meeting.

"Priest, have you found someone to replace Tiffany at the tattoo parlor?" King asked his brother.

Priest looked to Viper, his business partner at the tattoo

parlor, then responded, "No. We haven't been actively looking. Still trying to get over the shock of her death. We do still need to fill it."

King nodded. "If there is anyone out of the applicants we get, that looks like a good match, we will send them your way."

Priest nodded. "Thanks for thinking about us. Tabitha did mention that she was bringing her friend by to apply. If she wants it and looks like she can handle it, we will probably offer it to her."

"How about the bar and campground?" King asked. "We need to be critical in who we hire for those spots. Since we lost Tabitha at the bar, we are hurting. She really was pulling her weight there."

"What's with her going by Tabitha?" Baron asked.

"She's trying to better herself," Priest responded with a shrug.

"She came by the office and delivered breakfast for us from the coffee shop. She said Claire helped her get the job there?"

Priest nodded.

"Claire did all of that even though you and Tabby used to fuck?" Baron asked incredulously.

Priest's face turned to stone and Ranger shifted forward in his chair.

"Why would that bother Claire, *brother*? You know what type of woman Claire is. My past is my past, as it is for all of us. Tabitha's past is hers. Leave it be," Priest responded, the last part stated through gritted teeth.

"Nothing meant by it. Claire is a treasure. No doubt. Tabitha is another story in my opinion."

"Enough!" King said. "Let's get back to the business at hand," he added, glaring at both Priest and Baron, who was staring at Priest and then at Ranger who was staring Priest down. *Fuck me.*

"Let's move on to the next item," King pressed on. "Pretty."

"What about him?" Romeo asked.

"You are his sponsor. Do you think he is ready?"

"To patch in? Absolutely," Romeo responded.

"Let's put it to a vote," King announced, looking around the room.

The room was filled with ayes.

"Go get him then," King told Ranger.

Ranger grinned and left the room. A few minutes later, he came back with Pretty. Ranger sat down, leaving Pretty standing at the end of the table. No one would look at him.

King stood up. "Come here, son," he said gravely.

Pretty visibly swallowed and began walking to him slowly.

"You know, our father," King began, looking at Priest and then back to Pretty, "began this club with our uncle. If you look around this room, you see the pictures of the men who helped him begin this club. There are also pictures of the men who tried to take this club in a direction we didn't need to go. They wanted money by selling drugs and weapons. Whores. Is that what this club is about?" he asked Pretty.

Pretty looked at the pictures on the wall. He saw King and Priest's father. The man was known as Iron Back in the service because he would never bend his will if he felt what he was being asked to do was wrong. The warrior was in all of them. The club had been started as a place for men who were coming out of the service that needed a place to go. Whether it be to heal their physical or mental wounds. There had always been therapy, substance and alcohol abuse counseling. They had also been able to assist in job training or education. Pride welled up in Pretty's soul knowing what this club had given him and others.

Looking at King, Pretty nodded. "Yes. I know what this club is meant to be for the veterans and first responders that seek it."

King studied Pretty, then said, "Give me that cut, son."

Looking shocked, Pretty slowly took off his cut. Before handing it over, he folded it carefully, then handed it to King.

Romeo came up behind him. "*Brother.*"

Pretty turned to look at him and saw he held a new vest.

"Welcome to the table, *brother*," Priest added.

Pretty slowly reached for the vest. He looked at the front and back rockers. Picking up the vest, he placed it to his face and inhaled, closing his eyes.

"If this goes any further, I'm out," Viper said, smirking.

Pretty huffed a laugh and cleared his throat. Wiping his eyes and nose, he said, "Thank you, brothers. I can't even begin to explain how much this means to me." He shook his head at a loss for words.

"Don't dry your eyes yet. You're getting inked. Tonight. Right here!" Viper yelled.

"Sweet," Pretty said with a grin, still feeling a little dazed.

"Let's get out of here," King said to the group. "Adjourned."

They all left the room, heading to the main room. Claire was waiting when they got out there. She gave Pretty a hug and kiss on the cheek. Priest and Ranger scowled at her but she only stuck her tongue out at them.

"I'm so proud of you, Dave," she told Pretty.

"Thanks. That means a lot coming from you, Claire."

"You are a very important person in my life. You mean the world to me," Claire said, beaming at him.

"And we have a winner!" Romeo shouted.

"VIP?" Baron asked, grinning at Pretty.

"Ah, shit. Ah God no," Pretty mumbled, shaking his head and looking up to the sky.

"Oh no! I didn't mean..." Claire began.

"He's stuck with it now, Baby," Priest told her, wrapping his arms around her. Claire hid her face in his chest, laughing.

"Come on, man. I am your favorite person tonight," Viper joked, pointing over to the chair in the middle of the room.

Each of the club members took turns smacking Pretty's chest as hard as they could, leaving it red by the time Viper put the transfer on his skin. Priest and Viper would both take turns inking the club symbol onto Pretty's chest. Pretty looked down at the transfer and then frowned.

"The swelling won't mess this up will it?" he asked, looking between Viper and Priest, who had stopped what they were doing to look at his chest.

Snorting, Priest replied, "Hasn't that I am aware of before now…there's always the chance though," he replied with a shrug.

Pretty looked at him with a stricken look. "You wouldn't allow work like that to happen. Would you?"

Viper rolled his eyes and pushed Pretty back against the seat back.

***

Baron walked with Claire and Ranger to her SUV. Nate and Manda would be staying with her so the club could celebrate Pretty becoming a club member. Ranger planned on following her home and then coming back. With Anderson still out there, Claire still doesn't like traveling alone. Ranger and Priest were building a house further inland. Neither of them felt that Anderson had moved on. Baron was comfortable with the kids staying with Claire. He planned on having extra security on the house all night.

Baron kissed Manda on top of her little head. "I love you, baby girl." Looking over to Nate, he said, "Nate, take care of Manda and Claire."

"You know it," Nate responded, already buckled in beside Manda.

Baron gave Claire a hug. "Thank you, Auntie," he said quietly. "Drive safe."

Claire hugged him back. "I'll keep them safe."

"I know you will," Baron replied, looking her in the eye.

As Claire and Ranger left the compound, Baron returned inside for the first night he had had without the kids in months. The music was loud. Drinks were being served. Grinning at Otter, Baron headed over to the bar.

CHAPTER 10

The next morning, Baron woke up wishing he was dead. He didn't know which end of the bed was which. It hurt to breathe. He swore his pores hurt. He could have sworn he was trying to open his eyes but the room was still dark. Where the hell was he? *Oh fuck! Amanda!* With that last thought he attempted to get up and hit the back of his head against something.

"Ahhh fuck," he groaned. Breathing through the pain, he raised his head slower this time.

Where the fuck am I? Son of a bitch. He felt around with his hand. *Am I under the bed*?? With effort, he didn't know if he could stand, he pushed his head out from underneath the bed, realizing only his head was underneath it. Blinking a few times, he realized he was in his room at the clubhouse. The door to his room opened up and he rolled his head toward the doorway, having a brief flashback to when his CO would come in the barracks like that.

Shutting one eye, he looked closer at the figure in the doorway. No. It was much worse. It was his dad.

"Didn't even make it to the bed," King said, snickering.

"Did I die?"

"Nope."

"Life threatening wound?"

"Not even a papercut."

"Fuck me. My head. My mouth. My eyes. What the hell did

I drink?"

"More like what didn't you drink."

"Why are you still standing?"

"Self-control."

"Fuck me."

Shrugging, King offered him a hand up. Baron accepted it and everything went cartwheeling. His stomach most of all.

"Oh fuck," was all he got out before running to the bathroom.

Laughing loudly, King shook his head and left the room.

Baron heaved and heaved and then heaved some more. When he was finally able to stop the dry retching, he lay on the floor. The cool tile felt good on his hot face. After what felt like forever, he pulled himself up and dropped his clothes on the floor. Turning on the shower, he stood under the cold water until his teeth chattered. He turned it to warm and washed and then turned it back to cold and let the water wash over him. Stepping out of the stall, he toweled off and slowly got dressed. Reaching for the bottle of water and ibuprofen on his nightstand, he swallowed it down, draining the bottle of water. Stopping only to brush his teeth, he headed downstairs. There were bodies everywhere.

Baron sat down next to Romeo who grumbled, "Touch me and die."

"Dude. What. The. Fuck," Baron grumbled back, his head in his hands.

"I blame YOUR dad."

"He's YOUR prez."

"Son of a bitch. My eyelashes hurt," Romeo groaned.

"You stink too. It's coming out of your pores," Priest mumbled, sitting down to eat.

Romeo smelled himself and gagged. "That's where that smell is coming from," he said, getting up to stumble to his room.

"I hate myself right now," Priest groaned.

"You loved yourself last night," Ranger replied with a yawn.

"How could you let me drink like that?" Priest asked, looking at Ranger with indignation.

Ranger cut his eyes to his lover. "Seriously?"

"I'm telling Claire you let me do this. On the other hand, I may leave the country. She's gonna kill me all over again. I'm a dead man walking."

"Stop being dramatic," Ranger scoffed.

"How are you sitting up?" Priest demanded.

"I was in control. I didn't overindulge. I am good," Ranger beamed proudly.

"I hate you so bad right now," Priest said, putting his head in his arms on the table.

"Some of you guys still stink and need to go sleep it off. That does not mean out here in the open. Go to your rooms or find an extra one. Now!" King bellowed. "Anyone see the man of the hour?"

Ranger tilted his head back and laughed which in turn made Priest shoot a dirty look his way instead of just at King. He put his arms back over his head, groaning.

"Fucker," Priest could be heard saying.

"Dick," Ranger replied. He then looked at King. "Pretty is out cold on one of the picnic tables outside last I saw."

Rolling his eyes, King made his way outside, stopping to let someone in. The three men at the table looked over to see who was coming in. Tabitha and a girl they didn't know were bringing in coffee and bags of food. They both began setting the food out with plates, cups and utensils. Tabitha walked over to them.

"Well, two of you look like shit. Ranger, you and King look pretty good considering the night you all probably had."

Ranger huffed a laugh. "Yeah. I didn't participate as much as everyone else. We missed you last night."

"Yeah. I'm sorry I missed that. I was with my girl here. Everyone, this is Cassidy."

Cassidy gave them all a shy wave. She received three chin lifts in reply.

They all turned again to see King coming back in the building with Pretty, who kept going past them, straight to his room. Ranger looked at King with his eyebrows raised. They both snorted with laugher.

Tabitha looked over at King. "King, this is my friend Cassidy. I told you about her the other day."

King leaned over and shook Cassidy's hand. "Cassidy, it's nice to meet you."

"It's nice to meet you too. Tabitha has told me great things about the club," Tabitha responded, looking around at the large room. She noticed the bar area. The room was large with tables and chairs. There was a pool table and gaming system set up in front of a large sofa. The club's flag hung on the back wall. She nodded internally, she imagined this was a typical set up for the type of club.

King nodded in response to her statement about the club. "I understand you are looking for work?"

"Yes, I am."

"What skills do you have? I only ask because we have openings in several areas."

"I recently left a position where I cared for a child as a nanny. I have a degree in early childhood education. I'm also certified in first aid and CPR, as a home health aide with respiratory care."

King raised his eyebrows. "Wow. That is a broad range of skills. From children to adults?" he asked.

Cassidy nodded, looking at the man in front of her. He was groomed well. His hair was short and his beard was trimmed neatly. His eyes were ice blue. There was a strength about him that was present and undeniable. She had a feeling not much got by this man.

Bigs came back to the table and sat down, elbowing Baron

in the side. He received a grunt in response. After another push, Baron woke up and looked around.

"What?" he asked.

Bigs nodded his head toward King and Cassidy. Baron looked perplexed and shrugged his shoulders.

"Again, what?" Baron asked Bigs.

"Haven't you been listening?" Bigs asked, eyes wide.

"No," Baron mumbled, trying to lay his head back down on his arms.

"Jesus, man. She sounds perfect for what you may need."

Knowing Bigs, Baron sat up and slid his eyes Bigs' way. "You lost me," he replied, yawning.

Bigs shook his head at Baron and looked over at King, hearing King say, "It sounds like you are overqualified for what we need, honestly."

"Prez. You got a sec?" Bigs called out to him.

Looking over, King nodded and remarked to Cassidy, "I'll be right back."

"What's up?" he asked Bigs. The big man sat back with a big grin on his face, which made King narrow his eyes in suspicion. "What are you up to, son?"

"Sit down with us for a minute. I think we may have an offer for Cassidy, if she checks out."

King tilted his head to look at the man again but sat down in a chair. "Ok… what are you thinking?"

"Baron needs a nanny."

"What the fuck, brother?" Baron growled.

"Dude, seriously. Listen. You know you do. You are wearing yourself down. You are taking on too much at one time. You won't ask for help. You need it, brother."

"If this is about me bringing Manda to the office." Baron sighed, rubbing his face with both hands. "I'm sorry. I am a single parent doing the best that they can."

"Baron, respect. You know that is not what this is about. Not entirely. You can't give 200 percent all the time. You said it yourself. You can't keep doing this."

Baron looked over at Cassidy. She looked young. Had an athletic build. Blonde hair. Small tits. *Woah. Not going there. Can at least check her out. Not. No. Not that way.*

Baron called out to Cassidy, "Miss, can you come over for a minute, please?" *She looks nervous. Is that good or bad? Man, she smells good. No. No. No she does not.* "My name is Aiden Murphy. I am *possibly* looking for a nanny. More than likely, a live-in nanny. I have a nine-year-old and an infant. Do you have experience, references showing you have cared for children of varying ages?"

Cassidy looked at him and smiling, asked, "May I sit down?"

Flushing, Baron nodded and pulled out a chair for her. *Idiot. You know how to treat a lady.*

Cassidy smiled at him and thanked him. "I have experience in caring for children and the elderly. My degree is in Early Childhood Education. I can provide references and copies of my certifications andlicensure."

Baron sat with a pensive look on his face, chewing on his bottom lip. He noticed Cassidy's eyes flare at that. *No. That did not just happen. Nope, Baron you are losing it and out of your league.*

***

Cassidy looked at Baron and took a big breath. He was as intimidating as his father but she knew she was good at what she did. Steeling herself, she was shocked when Baron asked if she could come by his home to meet the kids. He wanted to see their interaction. She was about to suggest the same thing. Inwardly she nodded with respect for this man.

"Sure, I can come by. What is your address?"

Baron provided his address and added, "Bring your references, certification, and identification." Baron sat back and pinned her with his eyes that had gone from gray to ice blue like his father's. "Is there any reason why you can't work in the states, legally? Are you running from something?"

Cassie had been nodding at the last two questions, her eyes widened in shock. She gasped and sat up straighter, ready to flee.

Baron's eyes narrowed. "Don't lie to me," he snarled. "I will protect what is mine."

Jumping a little at the tone, Cassidy shook her head. "I wouldn't do that!"

"What is it then? Hmm? You are running from something. It's written all over you."

"My last employer's son," she began, faltering off and looking away, thoughts obviously going through her head. *How much do I tell him?*

"Hey, look at me. Are you in trouble? We can help if you are. Really. We will do that," Baron told her, softening his voice at the end. His eyes remained the ice blue, she noticed. She shivered.

Lifting her chin, she told him her story. "No. I left my employer when he passed away. His adult son had his younger brother put in an institution after that. I didn't have anywhere to go, so I contacted Tabitha and came here. Mr. Murphy, I love children. I miss the young man that I worked with, deeply. I need to work. What little savings I have is dwindling away. Please give me that chance to at least come by and meet your kids."

She waited, silently, holding her breath as he looked at her, silently.

Cocking his head to the side, he leaned forward. "You're running."

"I'm not. Not anymore," she replied, straightening her spine.

Her statement obviously surprised him. Watching her he

stood up and leaned across the table. "Come by tomorrow. 9AM. I don't know if this is for you or not," he replied as he walked away.

Cassidy watched him as he walked away. He left his scent of soap and man. Simple. She had a feeling the man was not. *Maybe this is a bad idea.* She realized that Tabitha was watching her, watching Baron, with a knowing look. Shaking her head, she turned away. She turned back to see Baron rap his knuckles on the bar and leave through the clubhouse door.

CHAPTER 10

Tabitha walked over to Cassie. "Well?"

"I go over tomorrow to see the kids," Cassidy replied.

"That's great! I'm sure you will see Baron too!" Tabitha said with a knowing look.

"Nope. Nothing like that can happen."

"But it could."

"No. This will be strictly professional."

"You would be living there though!"

"I know," Cassie mumbled, biting her lip.

Cassie could admit to herself that she found Baron attractive. Very attractive. She would have to be blind not to. He was guarded. She could tell he would pay attention to every detail. That didn't bother her. His questions did. She wondered about the reasons for him being so guarded.

"Just one thing," Tabitha said quietly, looking around. Seeing no one around she sat down beside Cassidy. "He has a wife. She had Manda and split. She was a terrible mother to Nate, Baron's oldest child. Baron loved her though. He had been overseas, since he was in the military and all. He has had the kids since he came back, all by himself. They don't know where his wife went."

Cassidy was shocked. How could a mother leave her children like that? "That poor man. How hard this must have been for him."

Tabitha scoffed. "Not a great homecoming for him. King had Nate for months until Baron came home. She left Nate at the library. LEFT. HIM. Crazy stupid bitch! Luckily, Claire was there. She called King. The rest is history," Tabitha said, letting her arms fall to her side. She had gotten pretty animated during the conversation, Cassidy noticed.

"Isn't Claire your boss?" she asked Tabitha, her brow creased.

"Yeah. She has been great. She really helped me get my life turned around and back on track. I wasn't very nice to her to begin with. I'm ashamed of how I acted now. I thought I was in love with Priest, her and Ranger's man, but I really didn't know him. It was never going to be what I wanted."

"Wow. This place has a lot of stories."

Tabitha laughed. "Girl, you don't know the half of it."

CHAPTER 11

The next morning, Baron heard a knock at the door. Looking at the monitor, he opened the door for Cassidy. They both stood there. Looking at each other.

Cassidy gulped and said, "Hello?"

Baron continued to stand in the hall, staring at her, with a stern look on his face. "You're prompt. On time. I like that."

"Baron, for heaven's sake. Invite her in," Cassidy could hear a voice from behind him say.

Baron jumped like he had been goosed.

"Claire, this is Cassidy," Baron said, looking between the women.

Claire walked to Cassidy and gave her a hug. Cassidy was surprised but returned the hug. She took in the tall woman before her. She was beautiful in simple white jeans and a blue top that made her eyes look like the Caribbean ocean. Her dark hair was pulled to the side and styled in a knot. Cassidy felt like she was in the presence of royalty from the stories she had heard. *No pressure. Nope. None at all.*

Placing his hand on Claire's back, Baron said, "Why don't we go to the living room to see the kids?"

Cassidy followed them into a masculine looking living room. Masculine except for the pink blanket and other assorted girlie items. She smiled. A boy standing in the middle of the living room turned to look at her. He looked exactly like his father except his hair was a sandy color.

"Nate, this is Cassidy. She is the lady I talked to you about," Baron said.

Nate looked at her. She could tell he was studying her, seriously. With a shrug, he simply said, "Hey." Then, "Auntie Claire, I think I figured out this recipe." He turned to Cassidy. "I'm learning how to make scratch made biscuits."

Cassidy noticed Baron turning his head to hide a smile. She didn't yet know how seriously Nate took his baking.

"I haven't had a homemade biscuit in forever," Cassidy told him. "Can I sit down and see your recipe?"

"Sure. The last ones I made were like rocks. I think I figured out what I did wrong," Nate said seriously, with his hands on his hips.

Cassidy looked over to Baron and saw him standing with his hands on his hips. Baron even had the same serious look on his face. She was beginning to think it was permanently there. She felt bad, instantly, for thinking that. She could imagine he was stressed and needed a break.

Cassidy looked back to Nate. Nodding her understanding, she said, "Hmm. I would like to see what you found."

Cassidy spent some time talking to Nate about his likes and dislikes. She was beginning to think that Manda didn't exist when she heard a cry through the baby monitor. When she looked over to Baron, she noticed he was staring at her, like he was trying to figure out a puzzle. Snapping out of it, he began to stand but Claire put her hand on his arm.

"If you show me where her room is, I can change her,"

Cassidy offered.

Baron rose from the chair, stopped, gave her the serious look again, grunted then left the room. Cassidy went with it and followed him down the hallway to a room to the right. He stepped aside so Cassidy could enter. Walking over to the crib, she peeked in. The most beautiful baby girl was looking back at her. Cassidy carefully picked her up. Turning, she gently lay her on the changing table. Cassidy began to talk nonsense to her. Manda stared back with the same serious look her father had. Cassidy snorted.

"If you put your hands on your hips you would look just like your father," Cassidy said, giving Manda a gentle poke to her belly on the last four words. Manda gave her a huge smile.

Cassidy finished changing her. Picking her up, Cassidy snuggled her and rubbed her nose in Manda's neck. She smiled at how sweet Manda smelled. Turning, she saw that Baron had left the room.

CHAPTER 12

Baron walked into his bedroom, shutting the door, and sat on his bed. Putting his face in his hands, he tried to catch his breath. He felt like he had been gobsmacked, watching her with Manda.

It was placed right in front of him. What his kids needed. A woman. A "mom" in their lives. Had he been selfish waiting this long? Had they been living a half – life? He didn't know the answers. He got up and quietly made his way down the hall. Walking into the living room, he saw Cassidy talking to Nate while giving Manda her bottle. Taking it all in, he cursed his soon to be ex-wife again. Their kids had a mother. He snorted. *A pathetic one.*

Nate looked up. "I'm kinda hungry. I'm gonna fix something to eat."

"If you don't mind, I would like to do that," Cassie offered.

Baron looked at her, tilted his head to the side a couple of times and left the room.

"I guess that means follow him to the kitchen. He really does know how to speak," Claire said, as she offered to take Manda.

Nate followed Cassidy into the kitchen. The kitchen, like the house, was modern and spotless. Cassidy ran her hand along the cool, marble countertop.

Turning to Nate, Cassidy asked, "So where can I find everything?"

Nate began opening the pantry and cabinet doors, explaining where everything was. By the time they had made it to the fridge, Baron gruffly spoke up.

"I could have shown you where the stuff is."

"I know. I wanted Nate's help," she replied.

Grunting, he left the kitchen. Claire passed him, rolling her eyes and sat down at the counter, out of the way. She did watch with a critical eye, the making of lunch. She was pleased with what she saw. Once Claire and Nate had lunch, Cassidy made lunch for Baron. With a tilt of her head, Claire indicated to go down the other hallway. Cassidy smiled her thanks and carried the plate that way.

Tapping on the door, Cassidy entered Baron's office. He jerked and looked up. They silently appraised each other.

"I brought you some lunch," she said simply, placing the plate on his desk. He grunted in response. Slowly, she turned to leave.

"Got it," she replied and left the room quietly.

***

Baron sat and looked at the sandwich like it was a bomb. He picked up the plate and sniffed at it then grunted. *Smells good.* He decided to go for it when his stomach growled. Picking up half the panini, he mused, *never used that panini maker before.* Taking a bite, he groaned and his eyes rolled back in his head. He took another bite. The bread was crusty, the turkey warm and the cheese melted just right. He looked at the sandwich again. There was a thin slice of granny smith apple. Then there was the spicy arugula and tangy mustard. He wolfed it down and munched on the chips, last, distracted. *Why is this going so well?* He shook his head. *No. Have to interview the others.*

He had gotten a few responses. None of them looked promising. Standing, he took the plate to the kitchen where Cassidy took it and washed the plate prior to drying it and putting it away. Baron looked at Claire, stunned. Claire in turn tilted her head to him with her brows raised.

"Did you make lunch?" he asked accusingly.

"I most certainly did not," she replied. "Give Cassidy credit where credit is due." Then she added, "I haven't heard a thank you yet."

Baron felt his cheeks heat. Only Claire and his dad could call him out on shit. "Thank you, Cassidy. Lunch was great," he said through gritted teeth, looking at Claire with raised eyebrows.

"Oh grow up," Claire huffed.

Nate giggled. Baron rolled his eyes to the sky with a why me look.

Cassidy cleared her throat and Baron's head snapped her way.

"Shit. Sorry. That will be all. Yeah. That's it. It was great. Yeah," Baron rushed out. *I sound like an idiot.*

"Thanks. Do you know when you will be making a decision? Also, what will the salary be and is there any paperwork you want me to complete?" Cassidy asked.

Baron looked at her. Blinked. Putting his hands on his hips, he stared at her some more. Finally, he responded, "I'm still working on that. You'll hear from me next week."

Cassidy nodded one and said, "Sounds good."

He was almost disappointed that she didn't have more questions.

***

Cassidy said goodbye to everyone and left. After getting in her car, she put her hands on the steering wheel and blew out a long breath. Pulling out of the driveway, her mind was full. She felt everything went well. She was already head over heels with Nate and Manda. Their father. That was another story. She wasn't sure what to do there. He was going to be a hard nut to crack. *But why?* Shaking her head she continued the drive home. She would have to put that and the worry aside until next week.

CHAPTER 13

Claire looked at Baron and tilted her head. "She's very good."

"She was okay," Baron murmured.

"I know this is hard, Baron. See how the other candidates are. See if the kids like them. In my opinion, she is the one. But, they are your children. You have to be the one that feels it is the right fit."

**

The next morning, the first lady showed up. She had oxygen that she pulled behind her. Baron opened the door and blinked. "Ma'am? Are you lost?" he asked politely. *Oh hell no. Please be lost.*

"I'm here (GASP) for the (GASP) interview," she replied indignantly.

"Oh. Did the ad provide you with the ages of the children?" he asked politely. Also confused.

"Yes."

"Umm."

"That boy doesn't run around a lot does he? I can't handle that," she added.

"Well, yes, he does. He's an active boy. He is involved in sports and enjoys being outside. He also enjoys reading and baking. My daughter will be moving around soon as well."

"That won't do. They can't do that when I am here."

Baron did a slow blink. Shaking his head, he responded, "Right. Um, I don't think this is the right fit. I'm afraid the answer is no."

"Asshole," she snapped. She turned and left, dragging her tank behind her.

Baron stood watching her, his mouth hanging open. "Well that was just great," he mumbled to himself.

An hour later, the second applicant arrived. Baron was taken by surprise. Harley, the applicant, was a dude. To be fair, Baron invited him in. He led Harley to the living room where King and Priest were sitting. They both looked at Harley and then at Baron. Baron in turn shrugged. Both men stood up. Harley turned around and left the house. King and Priest looked at each other, grinned, and then sat back down.

Baron had a headache. Going to the medicine cabinet, he took out some aspirin, dropping two in his hand then he popped them in his mouth to crunch them into bitterness.

"You won't find the answers at the bottom of the sink," King said from the doorway. He was holding Manda. She was holding part of King's beard in her hand. King let her yank on it, not a care in the world.

"Tell me about it," Baron grumbled. Looking back over his shoulder, he smiled at Manda. She beamed at him in return. "These are my babies, Dad. My kids. I could have lost everything with Nate while I was gone. I wish I hadn't stayed gone so long."

King reached out, placing his hand on Baron's shoulder. "You're here now, son. The past can't be changed. Live in the now.

And don't worry about tomorrow. Only what you can handle, son. You will be surprised at how much that actually is."

They both heard the knock at the door and Priest's response.

"Are those fucking track marks? Get the hell out of here!" They heard him yell.

Baron's headache was worse.

That afternoon, Ranger also stopped by. They were sitting at the kitchen counter, talking, when there was another knock at the front door.

"Hey!" a chipper girl in a tiny dress said.

"Hey," Baron responded, leaning against the doorframe. His dick twitched. *No. Not now. Bad dick.* "What can I do for you?"

She reached out and ran her hand down his arm. *So not helping.*

Clearing his throat, he croaked, "Ma'am?"

"Oh. I'm here about the job," she breathed. "Love your ink by the way."

"Oh. What's your name?"

"Chelsey."

"Right," he responded, scratching his head. "Follow me. I'm just having a small meeting with some of my club brothers. Don't mind them," he added, walking into the kitchen.

"Woah! Are they here all the time?"

"Nah, that's my dad. And these two are my uncles."

"Are any of you guys married?" she asked, batting her eyelashes.

Ranger snorted and shook his head.

Frowning, Baron asked her, "You are here about the nanny position, right?"

"Mm hmm. I'd be living here, right?" she asked, taking in the house.

"Not as the Mrs.," Priest mumbled, glowering at her.

King looked over at him and they both shook their heads.

Baron cut his eyes over to them.

"Ah, Chelsey, Kelsey…Chelsey! Got it! Manda is sleeping right now, but we could go meet Nate."

"Oh, maybe next time, when I start I mean."

"*Brother*," King said, with a murderous look in his eye. Baron shot a look back at him.

"So Chelsey, I don't think this is going to be the place for you. I'll walk you out."

Pouting, she gave a little finger wave to them and left.

"That is to be your type, from what I understand," Ranger grinned at Priest.

Priest dropped his head to the counter with a groan. "Never gonna live that down. Am I?"

"Nope," Ranger said with a grin, looking at King. They both tilted their heads back, laughing.

Baron walked back in. "Assholes," he growled.

"At least you still have her phone number," Priest laughed.

"BUT, now she knows where you live," Ranger added.

"Fuck me," Baron grumbled, rubbing his hands over his face.

"Looks like you have one option," King said, slapping him on the back.

"Yeah," Baron sighed. At least he had time to research her background over the weekend.

CHAPTER 14

Baron looked over the background check he had run on Cassidy. She had excelled in her studies and gotten a job right out of school with a wealthy family in Virginia. *This must be the family she mentioned.* The patriarch had passed, leaving the elder son in charge. Baron frowned. Why put the younger brother in a facility when he had Cassidy there to care for him? That didn't sit right with him. From what he could see, the boy had Autism. From the Social Services' records, the boy was doing well in school. He was thriving. *Something else then, but what?*

He sat back, rubbing his eyes and yawned. It had been a week. The sad affair of trying to find a decent nanny had come to an end. *Thank Christ.* Baron picked up the paper with her information. Taking a deep breath, he dialed her number.

"Hello," said a smoky voice. A voice that went straight to his dick. No. *No it did not. Not a chance.*

Clearing his throat, he croaked, "Cassidy?"

"Mr. Murphy. How are you?"

"Good. Um, good. Could you come by the house tomorrow? I'd like to go over all of the questions you had. If you agree, the job is yours."

Hearing her gasp, he almost groaned. *Jesus Christ. Want to hear that again. No. No you don't. She is the NANNY. Not happening.*

"I'd be happy to come by in the morning," she replied, sounding pleased.

"See you then. Good night," he replied, feeling better about the situation.

His dick was not feeling better. It was not going down or away. He couldn't remember the last time he had gotten himself off. Walking to the kid's rooms and checking on them didn't help. Not. At. All. *Fuck.* After checking the alarm system, doors and windows, he made his way to his bedroom. Pulling off his shirt, he stopped and then turned to lock his bedroom door. Shucking his shorts and briefs, he laid back on the bed, head against the pillow, he closed his eyes. Letting out a breath between his teeth, he took his dick to hand. Groaning, he increased the pressure as he stroked himself. He also varied the pace. Now that he was there, he wanted to stretch it out. Leaking precum, he began to thrust. *Oh yeah. This is what I have been missing.* Looking down, he began massaging his balls, then ran his hands over them and over his length, over and over. He moaned and threw his hand back to grip his headboard. Panting, he increased his speed, squeezing his tip, making his head roll back.

"Oh God, oh God," he said through gritted teeth.

His hips lifted and he was coming. Cum shot up his stomach and across his chest in spurts. Turning his head and biting down on the pillow, he milked himself, growling and groaning. After, he lay there, gulping in breaths of air, his chest heaving. With his clean hand, he wiped the sweat from his forehead. Looking over at the clock, he groaned. It was 1AM. Getting out of bed, he headed for the shower and washed quickly, then crawled into bed.

CHAPTER 15

Cassidy arrived at Baron's house promptly at 8AM. She knocked on the door and waited. When no one answered, she knocked again. Suddenly, the door swung open. Baron was standing there in shorts, holding Manda. Cassidy noticed several things at once. Baron had tattoos. He had a muscular chest and arms along with a trim waist. She was human after all. More importantly, she noticed the look of panic on his face.

He had turned away from the door and had gone down the hallway toward Manda's room. Cassidy closed the door and followed, alarmed at the look on his face. She walked into the room to find Baron sitting and rocking Manda, his face buried in her neck.

"Oh, my baby girl. You scared Daddy so bad!" she could hear him whispering to Manda.

"What happened?" Cassidy asked, coming over to rub the back of her head. *No fever. She's not fussy but obviously has been crying.*

Baron took a couple of big breaths and said, "She was choking." He huffed a breath. "Scared the shit out of me."

"My silly girl," he cooed to Manda. "Scaring Daddy like that!"

Cassidy smiled. "They tend to do that at times. Just when you least expect it."

Baron looked at her and smiled. "Yeah. I guess so."

Cassidy has never seen a more beautiful man. It took her breath away. To cover, she went to Manda's dresser to get out some clothes for her.

"What are you going to wear today, pretty girl?" she asked, looking through the outfits.

"She likes a bath in the morning. Well, at night too. Don't you baby girl?" Baron asked Manda, giving her a big kiss.

"Okay. Where is everything for that?" Cassidy asked, taking Manda from Baron.

Baron motioned for Cassidy to follow him to the bathroom. There, he took out toys, a washcloth, shampoo, soap, a diaper, and hooded towel. He also pulled out her baby tub and set it in the bathtub. Testing the water, he began filling the smaller baby tub. Turning, he began to say something but stopped when he saw the dumbfounded look on Cassidy's face.

"Yeah. I know. It's a lot. The counter is big enough. We could probably set the tub on that. I hadn't thought of that," he said quietly, his hands on his hips.

Cassidy found she was unable to speak. She got Manda undressed and gently placed her in the tub.

"That's my girl!" Baron said when Manda kicked her feet in the water. "I'm gonna make Nate some breakfast. He's gonna be late for school," Baron mumbled and left the bathroom.

Cassidy fanned herself after Baron left the bathroom. She giggled over Baron's messy hair and sleepy eyes. It made him adorable. She quickly cleared those thoughts from her mind and began bathing Manda. She picked up small toys for Manda to hold. Manda smiled and banged them on the side of the small tub. Cassidy looked at the tub and wondered if Manda should be moved to the normal tub with a bath seat, since she was sitting up. She decided to ask Baron about that. After carefully drying Manda off and getting her dressed, they both made their way to the kitchen.

CHAPTER 16

Baron stood in his room. He was looking at himself in the mirror. *Thank Christ I remembered to yank on my shorts*, he snorted at himself. *Good first impression? Maybe. No. Not. Idiot.* Chuckling to himself he headed into his bathroom to brush his teeth. Quickly getting dressed, he headed into the kitchen.

He stopped and quietly observed the scene in front of him. Manda was in her baby seat, watching Nate. Nate was shoveling what looked like oatmeal with berries in his mouth. Turning, he saw that Cassidy was pouring a cup of coffee.

"How do you take it?" she asked him.

"I'm sorry?" he asked, shocked.

"Your coffee," she replied, scrunching up her nose.

"Oh. Yeah. Black's fine. Thanks," he added, taking the mug.

"I can take Nate to school," she offered.

"Ahhh. What about Manda?"

"She can ride with us. I imagine, unless Nate rides the bus, we'll be doing that?"

"Hmm, yeah. Guess so," Baron mumbled, sipping his coffee.

He looked over at Nate and Manda and took a big gulp of

his coffee. *Why is this so hard?*

Setting down his mug, he placed his hands on his hips and began debating what could go wrong, how fast he could get to them if it did, and a dozen or so other things that could go wrong. He had another headache.

"Okay. Only if you take my truck. The base for her car seat is in there. Shit. I'll have to add you to the list of people that are allowed to drop off and pick up Nate." He took out his phone and made a note for himself.

Cassidy reached out and placed her hand on his arm. "Baron, I know this is hard. This is a big first step. I will be very careful with them. I would never do anything to place them in harm's way. I have a very good driving record as I am sure you have discovered. You are a thorough man. You have left nothing to chance. You can place your trust with me where they are concerned. Truly."

Baron looked at her, studying her. Trust did not come easily from him with good reason. He knew he had to take the first step though. With a deep breath, he nodded. Cassidy gave him the biggest, brightest smile he had ever seen, causing him to blink stupidly. He took her in. Blonde hair, blue eyes, tall athletic build. She was beautiful and strong. Perfect. Biting his lip he turned to look at his kids. They were his world. The only thing that mattered. He nodded again. He had to trust. Taking the last first step, he did.

"Nate, I will jot out a note for you being late."

"Okay, Dad. Can we go now though? I have a test."

"You do? In what?"

"History. I am good, Dad. I got this," Nate said, looking at him with a grin.

Baron grinned backed at him. He took in Nate, missing some teeth. He almost looked like a jack-o'-lantern. He would never say that out loud but the missing teeth made him laugh internally.

"You still should have told me," he said, narrowing his eyes at Nate.

"Sorry, Dad. Can we go? Please?"

Manda gave a slap on the little table. Baron turned to look at her with her hair darkening and her eyes so bright. His world. Just his world in front of him. Both of them.

Grabbing his keys, he walked out to bring his truck around. Nate hopped into the back seat as Cassidy placed Manda in her car seat. Baron looked at her.

"Hop in the passenger side. I need to lock up."

Cassidy huffed and got in the passenger side of the truck. Baron got in the truck after locking up and turned to her.

"I just need to do this today. You'll know the route and I can add you to the list at his school. And, I'll feel better," he added quietly.

She smiled at him. She understood completely.

CHAPTER 17

When they returned home, Cassidy took a sleeping Manda to her room and lay her down. Returning to the kitchen, she cleaned up the items from breakfast. Turning, she found Baron standing in the doorway. She smiled at him. He blinked and then gave a small smile back. With a tilt of his head he asked her to follow him to his office.

"We can go through the paperwork and terms for your employment," he said, as she followed him to his office.

Baron pulled out a chair for her and walked to sit at the desk. He gathered the contract and NDA, which she frowned at.

"I have a large security company. If you happen to see or hear something, I need to be sure that you won't say anything. Club business included."

Cassidy held his stare then went back to reading the document. Baron went over some other company business he had as she looked over the document. After a while, he noticed that she wasn't saying anything. Cassidy was staring at him. When he looked over, she snapped out of it. She noticed that he smiled and went back to his paperwork.

"Mr. Murphy," she began.

"Baron." He stopped her with a look. "Call me Baron."

"Okay…then call me Cass or Dee. Whichever you prefer."

With a raised eyebrow, he asked her, "Which do you prefer? It seems that is more important."

"Cass. Please," she added, looking down at her lap.

"Why not Dee?" he asked, curious.

"I just prefer Cass," she mumbled, not wanting to go into it. She wasn't sure why she added Dee. HE had called her that. Shaking her head, she looked at Baron and asked, "Baron. What will my salary and hours be?"

"Hours will vary, depending on my schedule. I'll be back in the office, so I'll be working 9 to 5 there. The thing is, I am on call all the time. I can guarantee Sundays off and possibly Saturday or a day during the week. You will have room and board, anything you need, free of charge. I'm offering $24,000 a year."

Cass gasped. "That's too much. Much too much!"

"I have to disagree. I have looked into how much daycare is. The hours that are expected go above and beyond what they can provide. I'm firm on what I am offering. Also, you will be using my SUV. I will drive my truck. That is non – negotiable. Your car is a bucket of bolts missing the handle."

Cass sat back, chewing her lip. She was torn.

"Cass. I need you to keep up with my children and my household. Cleaning and laundry are part of that. Cooking meals and even Nate's homework if I am not home. You will really be my right-hand nanny." He grinned at her. "You won't need to clean in here or my room. The yard work and trash will be taken care of. I hope you can tell that I like for the place to be kept neat and clean. I also prefer health food and snacks to be kept in the fridge and pantry."

Cass nodded, understanding the expectations. "Right-hand nanny? Never heard of that one," she said with a chuckle.

Baron chuckled. "Walk around the house. See where everything is. Let me know if there is anything you will need. Your room is upstairs, across from Nate's. You'll be able to tell the difference, I'm sure," he added with a shrug and smirk.

"I can do that," she said and left the room. She leaned against the wall and took a big breath. Nodding she headed for the stairs.

***

Walking up the stairs, she looked in the first room on the right. *Definitely Nate's.* She walked in and noticed the motorcycle posters on the wall. There were louvered shutters across the windows, letting the rays of sun in. Walking over, she straightened the camo sheets and blanket. She picked up a few items of clothes and placed them in the hamper. *Need to make a schedule.* Cass was pleased to see bookshelves on either side of his bed filled with books. His desk was a little messy. She left that alone.

Leaving the room, she noticed the bathroom. It has a double vanity, tub, and stall shower. She straightened the towels and tossed the one on the floor in the hamper. Leaving the bathroom, she walked into the room that would be hers. It was a simple room with a full-size bed that had a solid comforter. There was a dresser and closet. *Perfect*!

Making her way back downstairs, she checked on Manda and then looked at what was left of the downstairs. There wasn't much she wasn't already aware of, so she made her way back to the kitchen. She began preparing lunch for her and Baron when she heard Manda. Peeking in the room she saw Manda laying in her crib, looking at her hands, talking. Grinning, Cass walked over and scooped her up. She snuggled her and laughed at Manda's giggles. After changing her, she made the way back to the kitchen with Manda talking and singing the whole way.

***

Hearing Manda, Baron came down the hall and watched Cass from the doorway. *Tall. Legs are long. Runner's legs. Does she run daily? Her hips swayed. Tight ass.* She reached in the cabinet for glasses. *Small tits. Less than a handful. That's all right though. Those nipples are… ah fuck, Baron. No. Just no.* Adjusting himself, he sat down at the table. Sheepishly, he peaked at Cass. Sitting down. She smiled.

"Pasta salad okay? I added some fresh veggies and feta," Cass asked him.

"Huh? Pasta salad? Yeah. Good. Great."

She looked at him funny. Baron grinned and took a big bite of the salad.

CHAPTER 18

Cass spent the rest of the day taking Manda out for a walk in her stroller, doing laundry, and some light house cleaning. While Manda napped, she prepared a light snack for Nate. With that finished, she prepared a roast with red potatoes and placed it in the oven.

Baron had been holed up in his office since acting so funny at lunch. She hoped everything was okay. Going over the day in her head, she sorted and folded laundry. Nothing. Nothing stood out to her. Mentally shrugging, she began putting the laundry away. She could hear Manda babbling in her room. *Such a good baby.*

"Hello, pretty girl! Did you have a nice nap?"

Manda blinked at her then gave her a big, gummy smile.

Cass sang to Manda as she changed her diaper. Manda talked softly to Cass. Baron stood in the doorway, watching.

***

Standing, watching the interaction between Cass and Manda, Baron watched and wished that Manda's mother was the one taking care of their daughter. He frowned after that thought. The divorce would be final soon. After deeper thought, he realized that it wasn't Jade he wished was there, it was more that he wished that both his kids had a mother.

Cass turned around and yelped.

"Sorry! I just hadn't seen my girl all afternoon," Baron said, picking up Manda.

Cass smiled and looked at the two of them. "She looks like you," she murmured.

"Thanks, but she is prettier than me!" he said, looking at Manda. Manda patted his face. He grabbed her hand and gave it big smacking kisses, making her shriek with laughter.

But you are so fine. Cass wanted to smack herself on the head. *He is your BOSS*! Flustered, she straightened up the changing table and wiped it down.

"Cass, I'll get Nate today. Whatever is for dinner, smells great!" Baron said with a shy smile.

"Oh good! It should be ready at about 5:30?"

"Sounds good."

Handing Manda over, Baron nodded then backed out of the room, running into the door. Looking flustered, he left to get Nate.

CHAPTER 19

Nate came barreling into the house. "Hey, Cass! Hey, Manda Panda!" he said, giving Manda a big kiss on the cheek.

"Nah!" Manda replied and laughed.

"She almost says my name," Nate said with a grin, looking at Cass.

"How did you know to call me Cass? And go wash your hands. I have a snack ready for you," Cass said, laughing at the boy's energy.

"It just made sense to me," Nate said with a shrug and ran to the sink to wash his hands. "What are you cooking? It smells really good."

Baron came in the kitchen. "He's excited. Though I can't say that the volume will be any different at any other time."

Cass nodded and shrugged. "Kids can be that way."

Baron looked relieved.

***

As they ate dinner, Cass looked over at Nate. "I didn't notice how gold your eyes are, Nate."

He kind of squirmed in his seat and said, "Yeah, people say that all the time. They are like my Uncle Priest's eyes. I know that can't be. There is no way he was with my mom. They can't stand each other. In fact, he hates her."

Baron inhaled the water he was drinking and choked. Sputtering and coughing, eyes watering, he managed to strangle out, "Nate!"

"Sorry, Dad. People talk, but I know. She was not faithful to you. At. All. Can I be excused?"

Baron nodded weakly and put his head in his hands. *Where had that come from? Oh God. What must Cass be thinking?* Looking up, he saw a pretty blush on Cass's face.

"Sorry about that, Cass. I don't know where that came from," he mumbled.

Putting her hand on his, she said, "I'm sorry, Baron. I didn't know."

"Shit," he grumbled. "No. Jade did not sleep with my Uncle Declan. Priest is his club name. I know she slept with other men when I was overseas. Believe me, finding that out and knowing I had unprotected sex with her was not a great feeling. Then finding out she had gotten pregnant with Manda after that and then left her in a hospital in Virginia…"

"She did what?" Cass cried out, shocked.

"She left Nate at a local library and took off. Dad told me and I came home. A few months later, I got a call from a Virginia hospital. Romeo and I went there and picked up Manda. I've had DNA confirmed. She is mine. She's gotten a clean bill of health. So have I," he said simply, looking down at the table.

"Oh, Baron," Cass began.

The serious look had come back on Baron's face. He got up and left the table, heading back to his office.

That poor man. How betrayed he must feel. How hurt. Trust.

Now I get it. It will not come easily. What type of woman does that?? They are such great kids! Especially Nate! Wiping tears from her eyes, she got up to clean up the dinner plates.

***

Baron sat in his office, debating what to do about Nate. The only choice was to face it head on. Nate was a good kid in spite of everything he had against him. Baron was determined that his life with his kids would be better. Taking a fortifying breath, Baron headed up to Nate's room.

"Hey, Nate," he said, standing in the doorway of Nate's room.

"Hey," Nate replied, not looking up.

"Homework?"

Nate nodded.

Baron walked in the room and sat on Nate's bed. "Take a break for a minute." Baron thought back to the times his dad had done the same thing in his old bedroom. Shaking his head, he rubbed his jaw.

Nate looked over at him and put his pencil down.

"I wanted to talk to you about what you said at the table downstairs."

"Okay."

"First, I want to know where all of that is coming from. What did you mean about Uncle Priest and your mom?"

Nate scratched at a scab on his elbow and sighed. "I've heard people at the club. Kids at school. Some of the teachers. It's just talk."

Baron ground his teeth and looked away from Nate. "People will always talk. Especially gossip that is mean. Don't listen to them. You want to tell me who said those things?"

"Just Cowboy and some lady. I overheard some teachers when they didn't know I was there."

Baron saw red. *Fucking prospect is dead.* "Nate, I won't apologize for how your mom was when I was gone. I am sorry that I wasn't there. I'm sorry life was so shitty for you. I wish I had been there for you. I regret that I wasn't."

"It's alright, Dad. You had a job to do."

"I did but nothing will get in the way of me being yours and Manda's dad. Not again. I love you, Nate. I promise you that."

"Love you too, Dad."

"Come to me, if anyone, I mean anyone has anything to say? I mean it."

"I will, Dad. Promise."

"You are part of the best of me. Remember that. Always," Baron said, pulling Nate tight to him.

"I know, Dad. You're squishing the heck out of me, though."

Baron huffed a laugh. "You stink too. Go hit the shower, soldier."

"Yes, sir. I have to finish my homework though. I will get in the shower after that."

CHAPTER 20

After coming back downstairs, Baron looked in the kitchen. Seeing that it was clean and empty, he headed down the hall to Manda's room. Peeking in, he saw that Cass was rocking Manda and rubbing a finger over the baby's forehead. Cass looked up and then back down at Manda.

"Sometimes, or most of the time, doing this relaxes me," she whispered to him.

"I know what you mean," he whispered back. "Thank you, Cass. I hope you agree. I think this is going to work out."

Cass stood up and laid Manda down in her crib, covering her with a blanket. Baron walked over and gave Manda a kiss on her little head and ran his hand over her back. His heart filled with love all over again. Stepping out in the hallway, he found Cass waiting for him.

"Baron, I'd like to stay on. I agree. I think this will work out."

They both stood staring at one another. The energy between them was building. They could both feel it. They both spoke at the same time, breaking the spell.

"Good night."

"I'm gonna turn in."

They both bumped into and attempted to walk around each other, getting in each other's way.

Baron made it into his room and shut the door, locking it. He closed his eyes tight then opened them and headed for the shower pulling his clothes off. Turning on the water he stepped in the shower and closed the door. Leaning forward, one hand against the shower wall, he began stroking, quick hard strokes. He groaned at the friction. Resting his head against his arm, he began to pant. Thinking about Cass's long legs, imagining one wrapped around his hips as she stood in front of him, he began pumping into his fist. Soon it was like he was pumping in and out of her, faster and faster. Shutting his eyes tight he groaned, imagining him licking her long neck and her whimpering in his ear in turn. Throwing his head back, he came, coating the shower walls.

Leaning back against the shower walls, he tried to catch his breath. *Is this a good idea? Can I do this after all?*

CHAPTER 21

Cass sang softly in the kitchen. She was cleaning up the leftovers from lunch. Nate had a day off from school due to a teacher work day. He was in the den playing a video game and Manda was in her room napping. Putting the last of the dishes in the dishwasher, Cass looked up when she heard the doorbell. Checking the app on her phone, she saw that there was a delivery. She asked that the man leave it at the front door.

"Can't do that, man. It needs to be signed for."

Cass bit her lip. She didn't want to add having to go pick up a package to Baron's day. She began to text him asking if he had seen who was at the door when the voice came over the intercom again.

"Ma'am. I have other packages I have to deliver. I can't wait all day."

Rude was her thought as she looked at her phone. She made her way to the door only to scream when the door came crashing open. Falling backwards to avoid the door, she screamed again when the man came in, her phone went flying across the floor. Attempting to scramble away, her chin hit the floor when the man grabbed her feet and hauled her back toward the door. Looking up, she saw Nate standing in the doorway, looking terrified.

"Run! Get Manda!" she screamed. Nate didn't hesitate and ran down the hallway.

The man grabbed her by the hair and dragged her back into the room. She heard someone else come in the house. Her only thought was to fight. She swung her arms and kicked her feet. The man, who was average size, hit her across the face, causing her head to hit the floor. Seeing stars, things began to go gray.

"Cassie!" she heard Nate scream.

Nate was standing in the hallway, holding Manda. "Go, Nate! You know where to go!" she screamed at him as the man struck her again. Nate ran down the hallway toward Baron's room with Manda still in his arms. Turning, he looked back, and his face paled. Cass looked over at the second man and gasped.

"You! How could you?" she cried at the man as he tried to run past her. She grabbed his leg to slow him, knowing she would never be able to stop a man as big as he was. Still, the man fell against the wall.

"Get those kids! We need them!" the first man yelled.

Cass scrambled to her feet and pushed past both of them, taking them by surprise. The first man made a grab for her, slamming her against an end table, knocking the breath out of her but she still managed to escape the room.

"Don't hurt her!" the second man yelled, pushing the first man.

Cass crawled then ran to Baron's room. She felt her hair being yanked behind her and screamed. She kicked her leg out, made strong from years of running, and made contact with whomever was behind her. She heard a loud curse and was let go. Without looking back, she ran for the safety of Baron's room. Seeing Nate waiting in the doorway of the safe room, she sobbed and ran in, hitting the release for the door behind her, praying the men did not get in before the door closed.

CHAPTER 22

Baron had an alert on his phone and his blood ran cold. Running to the control room at his and Big's security company, he bellowed at the team, "What the fuck is going on at my house?"

"Sir, someone has broken in. Police have been notified and are on the way. The closest security team is also on the way," a young woman, named Ryan, told him.

"Fuck that," he roared as he ran from the room and out of the building.

Dear God please. Not my babies. Not Cass. He thought as he got in his car and went tearing out of the parking lot.

He pressed the phone to dial home. The phone rang several times and then nothing. Gritting his teeth he tried again, but this time he called the safe room.

"Baron?" a broken voice cried out.

"Oh God! Cass! Are you alright? Are the kids okay?" He could hear Manda screaming in the background. "Cass. I'm on the way. Do you hear me? I am on the way."

"Oh, Baron. Please. Hurry."

"Are you hurt? Are the kids hurt?" Baron yelled.

"We're ...fine. I think. I think the men are still out there. Please be careful!"

"I'm staying on the line until I get there. Do you hear me, Cass? Don't hang up!"

He could still hear them so he assumed Cass had heard him and understood. He could hear her talking to the kids.

"Oh Nate, come here. It's okay. I promise. Your dad is on the way." Baron could hear him crying. *Sonofafuckingbitch*!

***

Cass pulled Nate to her and held him in her one arm as she attempted to calm Manda in her other arm. She rocked back and forth with them, listening. She didn't hear anything outside the room. Nate soon got up and watched the monitors that showed the rooms of the house. He paced back and forth, looking at them. Getting up, Cass stood behind him and ran a hand over his back.

"There's my dad!" yelled Nate.

They both watched as Baron and Bigs made their way through the house, guns drawn. Bigs went upstairs while Baron handled the downstairs. They were thorough and quick but it felt like forever to Cass. Soon, they could see that Baron was outside the room. He entered a code and the door opened.

"Daddy!" Nate cried, grabbing a hold of Baron.

"Nate! Oh my boy! My sweet boy! Are you okay? Manda?" he cried, stepping in the room.

Quickly, he grabbed all three of them and held them in his arms. "Thank God. Thank God!" he kept saying. Looking at Cass, he saw that she had been hurt.

"Oh no," he said, voice husky. Touching her face gently, he pulled back as she winced. He swore and his hand formed a fist. "They hurt you," he stated through gritted teeth.

Cass nodded and realized her teeth were chattering.

"Baron! Son?!" a voice yelled.

"Here, Dad! We need Romeo. No one else comes in this house. Cass is going into shock."

"He's on the way," King said, stepping to the doorway of the safe room. "Nate? You good, son?"

"Yeah," Nate replied, but his face was very pale.

"The hell you are. Come on," he said to Nate, pulling him to him in a hug. Looking at Baron, he told him, "Give me her too," pointing at Manda. "We'll head to the living room for right now."

Cass handed over Manda. Baron pulled her toward him. She was in a full body shake now. He wrapped his arms around her and held her tight.

"Come on, baby. Come with me," he whispered.

Going back into his room, he lay her down on the bed and pulled a blanket over her. "Just lay down here. I will be right beside you."

She did as he asked. He brushed her hair out of her eyes and studied her face. Her eyes were glassy and her teeth were still chattering.

"Hey, Baron," Romeo said quietly, coming in the room and setting his bag down.

Cass jumped and cried out. "Hey, hey…Cassidy? It's Romeo. I'm a friend of Baron's. I'm also a nurse and paramedic. Can I check you out? Please?"

"Baron, can you step out? Just for a minute? Give her some privacy?"

"What the fuck, man?" Baron asked, irate.

"It's for her privacy. I need to ask her some things," Romeo said, holding his stare, not backing down.

Muttering, Baron left the room.

Romeo checked her pupils and blood pressure. Her eyes were glassy. *Not surprising considering what she just went through.*

As he began checking for injuries, she winced at the pressure he placed on her head.

"Yeah. You have a pretty good lump there. Your pupils are good. Nausea?"

"No. Just a major headache," she replied, wincing again.

Romeo placed his hand on her arm. "Cassidy, were you raped?" he asked, quietly.

"No. No," she responded again, shuddering.

"Okay. Do you feel comfortable talking about what happened? The police will have questions as well."

"I do have something to say. I'll tell you everything. I need Baron in here though."

Handing her an icepack, he gently lay her back on the bed and left the room.

***

Romeo walked into a room of very angry men. Baron looked at him, the question in his eyes and dread on his face.

"She wasn't, brother. She's pretty banged up though. She also wants to talk. She wants you in there though."

Baron was already down the hallway.

Cass looked up as Baron walked in. "Hey," she said, simply, holding out her hand.

Baron took it and sat beside her. He ran his hand over the top of her head carefully. He found he just had to touch her.

King also walked in the room. "Hey, Cassidy," he said, with a small smile on his face.

"Hey," she replied back, blinking back tears. She nodded when King indicated he was going to close the door.

"You're running on adrenaline right now, Cassidy. You will probably crash soon. What did you need to tell us?" King asked, slowly placing his hand on hers as he crouched down. "You won't be alone. I just want you to know that. Someone will be here the whole time."

"Thank you. That means a lot to me," she began, wiping tears from her eyes.

"Thank you, Cassidy. Thank you for saving my grandkids. There can't be enough we can do for you because of that," King replied, looking back at Baron. Baron nodded, squeezing her hand.

"That was all Nate," she replied with a small smile, pride in her eyes. "He got Manda and ran for the safe room. He was so brave!" she choked out.

Baron got up and began pacing the room, running his hands through his hair. "Those fuckers think they are going to come into my home and touch my kids?!" he roared. "My baby girl was crying. Screaming! She never cries! My God! Nate! Who is with them, Dad? Who is with them?"

The door opened suddenly. Priest stepped in and placed his hand on Baron's shoulder. Looking him in the eye, he said, "Baron, the kids are with Claire. Ranger and Pretty are there with them. Bigs too. Nothing is going to happen to them there. I swear it."

Looking at Cass, he nodded. "I'm sorry, Cassidy. This is some tough shit. You doing alright?"

She nodded and looked down. "I am ready to tell you what happened. Baron, please sit down."

Baron fumed but sat down and took her hand again.

Blowing out a long breath, Cass looked at them and began. "I was cleaning up after lunch when someone came to the door with a delivery. I asked who it was and was about to contact you, Baron, when the door burst open, knocking me down. The phone flew out of my hand. I tried to get away but they knocked me down again. I looked up, Nate, he…he was standing there. He looked so scared!" She paused here, taking deep breaths.

"We're here, Cass," Baron said, hoping to encourage her.

"Cass," King said, waiting for her to look over. "You have said 'they' a couple of times. How many were there?"

"Two."

"Did you recognize them?"

"One of them," she said, looking around.

"Okay. Who was it?" Baron asked.

She took a deep breath and looked directly at him. "Cowboy."

CHAPTER 23

The noise from the men in the room was loud and angry.

"What? Are you sure?" Baron asked, shocked. He grabbed her shoulders causing her to wince and him to flinch back, immediately contrite.

Shrinking back from him she nodded. She looked around the room, frightened.

"Enough!" King's voice rang out over the others. "Don't be frightened, Cass. Not of us. Never of us."

"Shit. Sorry, Cass," Baron said, sitting back down beside her, brushing her hair from her face, looking into her eyes. "I am sorry. I shouldn't have yelled or grabbed you. Forgive me?"

She nodded, tentatively. He felt even worse.

"Do you guys need to hear any more?" she asked, quietly.

"Please keep going, Cass," King said, quietly thinking, arms crossed across his chest.

"I was struggling and fought against the other man. He was yelling at Cowboy to get Nate and Manda," she recalled. She and Baron were both shaking, but for very different reasons.

A fury was building in Baron, the likes he had never felt before.

He was breathing hard, fists clenched.

"No. No, motherfucker. Not my kids," he said, looking to Romeo. "You vouched for him! You sponsored him," he spit out through gritted teeth.

"I did, man. I…I don't know what to say. Never saw this. Didn't know!"

Baron roared and put his fist through the wall.

"My kids! He tried to touch my kids?! Take them? He's dead! The guy with him? Dead."

King and Priest grabbed him.

"Stop, son! Stop! You're scaring Cass!" King roared.

"He was a brother," Baron said, dropping to the bed, his head in his hands. He looked up at King. "They're my kids, Dad."

"We are going to get him, son."

King looked to Cass. "You didn't know the other man?"

"It was Mr. Anderson and Cowboy," Nate said, from the doorway.

They all turned to look at him.

"He is a dead man," Priest solemnly vowed.

King whipped around to look at Nate. "Be sure, Nate. This is important."

"I am Grampa. I am," he said, looking at King.

Baron pulled Nate to him and hugged him. He put his face in his hair, smelling his shampoo and Nate's little boy smell. Closing his eyes, he thanked God they were all okay.

"Guys, Cass needs rest," Romeo told the group. "Cass, I can't give you anything to help you sleep with your head injury. I'll come in to check on you every once in a while. Okay?"

"Oh. I don't know. What if the kids need me?" she said, trying to get out of the bed.

"Rest. The kids will be with me," Baron said, putting his hand on her shoulder. *He called me baby.* "Okay," she agreed, laying back against the pillow. "Thank you, Romeo. For everything."

Giving her a small smile, he followed the others out of the room.

Cass lay back on the pillows that smelled like Baron. The scent was woodsy and crisp. With a sigh, she fell asleep.

CHAPTER 24

She dreamed of him. Baron. He called me baby. She smiled, letting the warmth of that statement wash over her. Cass was a virgin, but in her dream she was with Baron. He kissed her so sweetly and held her. Then, the kisses became more demanding. Not surprising that the change came like a slow burn with this man. They fit together so perfectly. Baron ran his hand up her stomach and cupped her breast, tweaking her nipple, making her gasp. She moaned and arched her back.

"So beautiful, my Cass," he murmured. 'My Cass', she thought. The statement made her feel safe.

Nuzzling her neck, he moved down to her chest, sucking her nipple into his mouth. He licked and sucked at the other, giving it equal attention, making her cry out.

"Baron! Please!"

She didn't know what she needed, but was sure he did. Wouldn't he, though? He had more experience than she did.

"Cass, please say you want this. Say you want this with me," Baron whispered.

"Yes, Baron. Only with you!"

Cass awoke to a dark room, curled into a body next to her. She sought out the warmth from this body in her sleep. An arm came around her shoulders and pulled her closer. Cass nuzzled into the man's chest. Baron, she thought sleepily.

"Baron!" she screeched, sitting up so fast her head began to swim.

"Cass, you okay?" Baron asked her sleepily.

"What am I doing here? Where am I?" she asked.

Alarmed, Baron sat up and turned on the lamp.

"Cass, how far back do you remember? Shit. I'm calling Romeo. Maybe I should take you to the hospital? Oh my God. Can you get amnesia after being okay, but then going to sleep? That sounds ridiculous. Cass, are you going to answer me? Fuck me. What the hell." He said all of this frantically.

Cass sat staring at the man. Shaking her head, she began to laugh. She rolled on the bed holding her stomach.

"Should I add hysteria to amnesia?" Baron asked, his mouth twisting to the side.

She wiped at the tears running down her face and snickered. "Oh, Baron. The look on your face. I don't think I have ever seen you anything but composed. You…you," she began, but started laughing again.

Serious Baron was back, hands on hips. Frowning.

"Your hair is sticking up everywhere! You were, fre…fre... freaking out!" she managed to get out.

"Yeah. Yeah I was, Cass. It scared me!"

Attempting to compose herself, she rolled off the bed, scaring Baron to death, and walked into the bathroom.

"Cass!" he growled, at the door.

"Baron! I have to pee!"

Running his hands through is hair again, he growled, "Woman!"

He heard the water running, then the door opened.

"What?" she asked, hands on her hips.

She was beautiful. Hair mussed, her faced flushed from laughing. She took his breath away.

"You okay?" he asked, voice gruff with emotion.

Shivering, she nodded.

"Good. Yeah. Good. I'm going back to sleep," he said, stepping back from her, looking away.

"Oh. Yes. What time is it? Manda should be up soon," she replied, looking at the clock. "4AM. I'll head up to my room to get another hour or so in."

"Sounds good. Pretty is in the living room. Don't be alarmed when you see him. Otter will be here to relieve him around 7," Baron added.

"Oh good. That's good," Cass agreed, nodding and heading to the door, quietly she closed it.

Cass headed up the stairs quietly and went straight to bed, dreamless.

***

Baron fell back on his bed, groaning. He had almost kissed her. Again. All he could think about. Not act on. No. Not act on. Rubbing his hands over his face he blew out a puff of air.

It was just the emotion of the past day. Nothing more. It couldn't be. He needed her for the kids way too much for there to be anything else and jeopardize that.

He didn't even bother trying to go back to sleep. Getting up slowly, he began to get ready for the day.

CHAPTER 25

The two men sat talking in the kitchen of the house two counties away from the club. Distance was best for now. Things could have gone better trying to get that girl and the kids. They both heard a car door and feet stomping to the door.

Cowboy rushed to the door, gun drawn. He opened the door as Sasha came storming up to the door. As she went past him, he stepped outside looking around. She was alone. Heading back into the house he heard raised voices.

"You tried to kidnap that girl AND my grandkids?" Sasha shrieked.

Anderson looked at her calmly. "Shut up. Do you know what a girl like that can get on the market?"

"The market?" she asked, arms thrown out wide.

"Yeah. The. Market. Get a clue, you cheap bitch. This lifestyle you have become accustomed to isn't cheap."

"I couldn't care less about that girl. My grandkids are off-limits!"

"You couldn't care less about them. Stop the act. The boy could bring a decent purse. The baby though. Do you know what the right buyer would pay for her? I would be set between her and the babysitter."

Sasha looked at him and paled. Launching herself at him, she shrieked. "You won't touch them! You pig!" she screamed, raking her nails down his face.

Anderson roared in pain. Putting his hand to his face, it came away with blood. Snarling, he turned on Sasha. With a backhand, he knocked her to the floor.

Moaning, she crawled backwards away from him and looked to Cowboy for help, her eyes pleading. Cowboy turned away from her, eyes closed, fists clenched.

Anderson slowly kneeled over her and reached for her throat. With his other hand, he pushed his hair out of his eyes. Eyes that Sasha had found so beautiful before, now they were cold, dead.

"You knew your place in this. You are replaceable. You were a means to an end. That end is now," he said calmly, looking at her. Placing his hand around her throat he squeezed and watched as she turned red. Her eyes bulged. He smiled coldly as her feet kicked and she beat at his arms with her hands, clawing at his hand. Her efforts were like pats from a baby. She tried to buck him off, kicking her legs harder. Her struggles soon lagged. Anderson watched closely for the light to go out of her eyes. He was so hard. Sasha had stopped breathing. One hand still rested on his arm. He batted it away, listening with pride as it made a loud thunk against the floor.

Turning to look at Cowboy, he smiled. "You know where to leave her."

Cowboy nodded slowly, his face haunted.

"Now isn't the time for regret. They brought this on themselves," Anderson said, looking down at Sasha. "King should have minded his own business. Priest and Ranger took what was mine."

Cowboy shuddered. He looked to the doorway and wondered how it had gotten this far.

CHAPTER 26

King's party in honor of his retirement from the fire department was going strong. He couldn't believe the amount of people that were there. There were club members from Tennessee, former partners from the fire house, and people who had been saved through his actions over the years. It was humbling. He looked around at his club house and smiled a little. The pride he felt was a good feeling. They were still building but he knew they would be stronger despite what had happened over the past two years. He took a long pull from his beer and sat back against the wall listening to his cousin Cain tell some story that sounded totally made up, but he laughed anyway. The guy just brought it out of him.

Otter ran into the clubhouse, looking for King. A couple of people stopped what they were doing to stare.

"Where's Prez?" he asked.

Everyone looked around. "Hey, Prez! Killian!" someone yelled.

King looked up and saw the stricken look on Otter's face and walked over to him. Dread filled his gut.

"What's going on?" King asked, setting his bottle on the bar.

"Prez. Shit, man. There's a car…Oh God, Prez," Otter attempted to speak a few times but obviously was out of breath.

"Just say it, man!"

"It's Sasha's car. There is a body in it. The police are there."

"Where is 'there'?" King asked in a low calm voice.

"About five miles down the road. I saw Ranger there and some other cops."

"Fuck. I'll be back. Do not let Baron know. Not yet!"

King left the club quickly, got on his bike and roared off out of the club grounds.

***

Baron stood on the other side of the room, observing King and Otter's exchange. When he saw King run out, he frowned. Finishing his beer, he walked toward the door. The place was filled with people. Everyone seemed to want to stop him to talk, so much so that he lost track of Otter. He had a bad feeling in his gut.

He could hear sirens in the distance. Fearing what that meant, he got on his bike and went in the direction of the sirens. Baron slowed as he came up to the scene. He saw three bikes parked on the side of the road. Pulling up behind them, he parked and walked up to a deputy who was directing traffic.

"What happened?" he asked Henderson, a man he had gone to school with.

"Dead body. Found in a car," Henderson replied. "You can't go any further. They'll have my ass."

Baron had stopped listening. A person had moved, so he had a view of the front of the car. Off to the right, he saw King, squatting down, his head in his hands.

"Dad?" Baron called.

King's head snapped up. Slowly, he stood and made his way to Baron. Another person moved and Baron could see the person in the car. His mom. Sasha. She wasn't moving. He broke past Henderson.

"Mom!" he yelled, running toward the car.

King caught him and held onto him, turning him away from the car.

"Dad? Is that Mom?" Baron yelled, struggling against King. He could see Priest running to them. He then saw Ranger looking over at them, then bark something at another deputy.

Priest reached them and held onto both of them. "Uncle Dec, is that my mom?" He felt calm but the last word faltered.

"She's gone, son," King said into Baron's neck. "I'm so sorry. Your mom's gone."

That last word shattered Baron.

"No!" he roared. "Call an ambulance! Where is Romeo? He will know what to do!" he yelled as he began fighting against both men. "Let me go! I want to see her!"

"No, son! You don't! Stop fighting us!" King implored him.

"Let me go! Sonofabitch let me the fuck go now!" Baron roared to the sky.

Suddenly, Ranger was there in Baron's face. "Listen to me! This is a crime scene. You cannot be there, Baron. I'm sorry, man. Truly I am. Your mom is dead."

Baron moved back from all of them, his hand over his mouth. He turned away, feeling sick, lost.

King walked up to him and pulled Baron to him, wrapping his hand around the back of his neck and rested his forehead against his.

"Why are you on the scene, Ranger?" Baron asked, almost too quiet to be heard.

"I'm sorry, son. It wasn't a natural death. She was murdered,"

Ranger responded, looking him in the eye.

"But...I can't believe this. Who would do that? To my mom?" Baron said to no one in particular.

Priest glared at Ranger. They knew. King did as well. Anderson.

"We're going to find out. I swear to you. We will," Ranger said solemnly.

CHAPTER 27

Baron and King sat in the living room of King's house. They were silent. Their ride to the house had been completed in the haze of disbelief.

"Was she shot?" Baron asked, looking at the floor.

"No," was all King said.

"Do they know how she died?"

King didn't respond.

"If they don't know, Dad, why was Ranger there? It wasn't a wreck from what I could see. It could have been her heart or...or," Baron knew he was grasping but the truth was just too horrible to comprehend.

"She was strangled," King said quietly, looking at Baron.

"What?" Baron asked, shocked.

"Someone strangled her and left her there for us to find her," King replied, fists clenching and unclenching.

"Why would they?" Baron began, then faltered. They knew why. They knew who.

Baron watched as his Dad walked out the back door of his house. Laying his head against the back of the chair, images of his Mom raced through his head. He reflected back on his time with her. Her mothering style had been very similar to Jade's. She had been meant to be on the back of a bike not for motherhood. Baron knew she had done her best and he loved her for it. He would miss her all the same.

The front door opened. Priest and Claire came in. Baron stood and accepted Claire's embrace. He suddenly felt hollow and very tired. He knew it was just the beginning. The house and yard would be filled with people soon. He suddenly wanted his kids. Wanted to hold them. Be close to them.

Looking past Priest at the door, he asked, "Where's Cass and the kids?"

"She took them home. She knew you needed time. Time with your Dad," Claire told him, rubbing her   hand on his back.

Baron rolled his head around. He was neck was stiff. His whole body tired. "Tell Dad I will be by later. I need to be with my kids," he said simply.

Priest stopped him. "You okay to drive?"

Baron nodded.

"Ranger will come by when he can. He'll probably come here first."

Baron found himself in an embrace. Shocked, he returned the embrace. The man embracing him was Priest, the man he butted heads with and sparred with over club business. This. This was his Uncle Declan. He was grateful for it.

***

When Baron reached his home, he walked in the house and paused, listening. His security team was posted outside. He could hear Nate upstairs in his room. Walking to the bathroom, he leaned against the wall, emotion washing over him. Cass was giving Manda a bath. Manda was sitting in the bath seat that he and Cass had argued over. Baron had been unsure if Manda was ready for it. Seeing her splashing and picking up toys made him shake his head. Such a silly thing to worry over. Quietly, he made his way to his bedroom, shutting the door. Sitting on his bed, he placed his face in his hands and let the tears quietly fall.

Cass saw Baron out of the corner of her eye. Her first instinct had been to run and wrap her arms around him, but she sensed his emotions were too close to the service. She finished bathing Manda and put her in her jammies. Cass grieved silently for the man and his children. *Haven't they been through enough?* As she prepared to give Manda her bottle, she saw Baron standing in the doorway.

"Hey," she whispered.

"Hey. Nate's already in bed. Do you mind if I....?" Baron asked, holding out his arms.

"Of course," Cass said, handing Manda to him.

Manda smiled and rubbed her eyes, laying her head on his chest. "Hey, little angel. My pretty girl," Baron said, lifting her to give her a kiss. He nuzzled her hair, smelling her sweet scent. He began quietly talking to her, telling her how much her gramma had loved her and how she always would.

Cass listened quietly outside the door. She left for the kitchen when the tears began falling. Baron sounded so broken talking to Manda. Not long after, she looked up to see Baron standing in the doorway.

"I'm going to my room. Do you," he paused. "Do you mind sitting with me?"

"I will, of course I will."

They walked to his room, where Baron looked around awkwardly. "I'm not sure why I asked you to sit with me."

"Here," she said as she sat against the headboard. "Put your head in my lap."

Baron stared at her, looking perplexed. Shrugging, he crawled onto the bed. Laying on his side, he put his head in her lap. She rubbed his temples and smoothed his hair. He never spoke. At first, he was stiff, but gradually he began to relax. Soon, he was asleep. Gently, Cass moved out from underneath him, but he kept an arm firmly around her. At a loss, she eased back against the pillow. At some point, she fell asleep.

***

The next morning, Cass felt someone brush her hair back. She gradually opened her eyes to find Baron staring back at her. Neither said anything. Their hands lay side by side. She noticed how clear his eyes were. *Beautiful.* He noticed a sprinkling of freckles across her nose. *Adorable.* Neither wanted to move. They didn't want the spell to be broken.

"Dada," they heard a tiny voice say.

Both of their brows creased in confusion. Where was that voice coming from? Quickly, their eyes widened and they were scrambling out of the bed, racing to Manda's room.

"Hey, Princess! What did you say?" Baron asked, swooping Manda up.

"Such a clever girl!" Cass praised her.

"Da!" Manda cried.

"Yes! That's your Daddy," Cass said with pride, running her hand over Manda's head.

"What's going on?" a sleepy Nate croaked from the doorway.

Baron looked over at him, his smile fading. "Hey Nate," Baron said, handing Manda over to Cass. "I need to talk to you. Can you come with me?"

Nate visibly swallowed. "Did I do something?"

"Not that I am aware of. Come on."

Nate reluctantly followed Baron to the living room.

"Sit down. Come on," Baron said, motioning for him to sit down.

Nate looked at him and sat down.

"Nate," Baron sighed, swallowed and looked back at him. "Yesterday, um, yesterday...fuck this is hard," Baron paused, then began again. "Nate, Gramma Sasha died yesterday."

Baron finished the statement and thought back to his reaction to his Dad the prior day. The shock. The denial. Cussing him. He looked at Nate, gauging his reaction.

Nate quickly swiped his eyes with his arm. "Did you say Gramma died?" he asked in a squeaky voice.

"Yeah, buddy. I did," he said softly.

Nate looked at the floor and chewed his lip. "What about Grampa?" he asked, his chest hitching.

"He's fine. He's home. We will see him later today."

"Is he sad?" Nate asked, picking at the sofa.

"Yeah, he is."

"Are you sad?" he asked in a small voice.

Baron looked at Nate. "I'm real sad."

"Can I be sad?"

"Yeah, yeah. You can be sad. You can feel anything you want right now."

Slowly, Nate crumpled into Baron. He sobbed and wrapped his arms around Baron. Baron held him and wiped away his tears. Cass stood holding Manda, watching them. Walking over, she sat down with Manda and wrapped her arms as far as she could around the three of them. She murmured small comforting things to all of them. In time, Nate turned and held onto her and slowly, his crying eased, until there were only hitches coming from his chest. Cass still held him and Manda, singing softly.

As Baron locked eyes with her for a second time that morning, it all fell into place. She was the one for him.

CHAPTER 28

The funeral was a somber affair. Ole Red, one of the former club members from the now closed North Carolina chapter, read scripture and shared stories of Sasha's younger days and her days with King and after. She had always been good to the club. King sat, Priest on his left and Baron on his right, Nate at his side. Claire sat beside Priest. Ranger behind Priest and Romeo behind Baron. Cass had stayed home with Manda.

The people who came to pay their respects lay red and white roses on the casket as they passed. King said nothing. As the last person passed, King stood up, turned and stopped in front of Dany, the librarian who Claire had worked with, with his hand out to her. She stood, took his hand and they walked off to his car, his arm wrapped around her the whole way. Baron and Priest both shot looks of, 'what just happened? And 'did you know?' Priest shrugged and looked at Claire who had a very pleased look on her face.

***

Claire had offered to pick up Cass and the kids, so she left next. The rest of the group was meeting at the club. Walking up the walkway, Claire found it odd that no one from Baron and Bigs' team was parked in front. There was a van parked on the street but no one was in it. As she came closer to the doorway, the hair on the back of her neck went up. The door was ajar.

She began to pull out her phone, when she heard Manda's cries. She sounded terrified. Cursing, Claire ran for the door and into the house. Rushing into the living room, she saw that a chair had been turned over. The coat Claire was wearing had a concealed pocket. Claire pulled her.380 out from this pocket. Keeping her arms in front of her, gun ready, she made her way further into the house. She could hear a struggle coming from the hall with Baron's office. Manda's cries came from her room. She turned the corner to Baron's office and gasped. Anderson had Cass bent over Baron's desk, a syringe in her neck. He removed the syringe and Cass slumped to the floor.

"Get away from her!" Claire cried out.

Anderson looked up, startled. Then he smiled, the eerie smile he always had for Claire. It was the same smile he would have for her when he had her locked in the trunk of the car. Claire shuddered but she steadied her aim and pushed down the revulsion she felt.

"My heart. You've come back to me," he said as he pulled out a second syringe. Slowly, he made his way around the desk, never taking his eyes off Claire. "You look beautiful. I never approved of you changing your hair color before. Have you learned some respect?"

"Fuck you!" she spit out. "Respect this. Come any closer and I will end you!" she added through gritted teeth.

He tilted his head and tsked. "No, no. You won't speak to me that way," he said, shaking his finger back and forth.

"I WILL shoot you. Do. Not. Come any closer."

A look of fury came over his face. "Thankless bitch! I would have given you everything!" he yelled and charged.

Claire pulled the trigger. He kept coming and lunged for her. Falling back into the wall, they struggled. He attempted to choke her, cutting off her air, but she still held onto the gun and pulled the trigger again and again. Looking into his eyes, his rage turned to shock.

"Bitch!" he spit out. "You don't get to kill me," he said as blood and spittle flew out his mouth.

Leaning forward, she got in his face. "I just did."

She watched as he stumbled back. Stopping, he looked at the blood on his hands from gripping his mid-section and fell to his knees. More blood came out of his mouth and he fell forward. Everything sounded funny to Claire and all she could smell was gun powder. Stumbling back against the wall, again, she slid to the floor. *Shock. I'm going into shock.* She stared at Anderson, waiting for him to move, like a bogeyman in the movies.

Hearing a noise, she looked to her left and saw Cowboy standing at the end of the hall. Sucking in her breath, she turned and aimed her gun. Pulling back the slide, she aimed at him.

"Long time no see, Claire," he said casually.

"Cowboy. Do not come down this hall!" she yelled back at him.

"Where's Anderson?"

"He's in there." She motioned with her head.

"They why are you out here?" he asked, reaching behind him.

Cowboy's head whipped up to look at her and she fired hitting the wall beside where he was standing.

"Stupid cunt! You missed!" he snarled.

"No. I didn't. That was your warning. The only one you are getting," she said calmly. "I won't miss next time. Leave. Now!"

Cowboy began to slowly retreat backwards. "You know this ain't over, right?"

Claire didn't respond. When she was sure that he was gone,

she got up. Stepping over Anderson, she went to Cass and checked her pulse and breathing. She seemed okay so Claire ran to get Manda. Picking up the baby, she cooed and tried to comfort her, holding her close. Hearing car doors, Claire ran around the corner, stopping suddenly. A patrolman was standing there with his gun out.

"Put your hands up!" he barked.

Claire, holding Manda, nodded. "I need to put her down. Her high chair is here in the kitchen. Can I set her there?" she asked, motioning with her head toward the kitchen.

"Slowly," he warned.

Nodding, Claire made her way to the high chair and placed a still crying Manda in it.

"Shut that kid up!" the patrolman barked.

Claire winced and looked back at him incredulously.

"We got two bodies in here," a voice yelled from Baron's office.

"She needs medical attention," Claire told the patrolman.

"Quiet!" the patrolman barked.

Another patrolman came in from the hallway. "Guy was shot three times. DOA."

"The other body?"

"Unconscious. There's a syringe beside her. Get this, I think the DOA is Brent Anderson."

They both turned to look at Claire. "He was going to hurt her. He injected her with something," Claire tried to explain.

"I told you to SHUT. IT," the patrolman responded to her. Then the patrolmen looked at one another and then back at Claire. "How did that blood get on your hands and on the baby?"

"He was coming at me with another syringe. He kidnapped me last year."

"You shot him?"

Claire looked at him but said nothing.

"That's all I needed to know," he said, walking toward her.

"What?" Claire asked, but the patrolman slammed her face first onto the table. Claire cried out from the impact.

The patrolman leaned over her. "You are gonna pay for this, Claire. Anderson was my friend. You won't be getting out of this one so easily." After that he pushed her injured face into the table harder, making her cry out again.

Hauling her to her feet, she stumbled. "Get up. Lazy bitch."

"You. You are going to be the one who pays," she managed to get out.

"You? You. Threatening me? Me?" that patrolman laughed.

***

Walking out of the house, Claire could see that the house was surrounded. She heard a bellow of rage but was too dazed to see who it was.

"No! Goddamn it! Let her go! I'm a cop. I'm a cop. That is my wife! Get the fuck out of my way!" a voice bellowed. Ranger had gone crazy, trying to get to Claire. He was fighting anyone that was trying to stop him from getting to her.

"Sir! You need to calm down!" a patrolman yelled him.

At this point, it took six men to take Ranger down. "Get your fucking hands off me! My name is Detective Wilkes!" The rest of his rant was cut off as knees began hitting him in his lower back and kidneys, causing him to roar in pain.

"Get the fuck off him! Is this how your treat one of your own?" Romeo roared as he tried to show his credentials to be let in for Cass and Manda.

"Taylor? What are you doing here?" another paramedic yelled his way. "We got this. Possible overdose."

"No. No way!" Romeo yelled back at him. "Not happening!"

Baron could also be heard yelling from the crowd. "Let me through. This is my house!" he yelled at the deputy at the line of people. The deputy looked at his ID and let him through.

A woman was walking out of the house holding Manda.

"That's my daughter. Give her to me!" he roared at the woman, grabbing Manda. Manda cried and lay her head on Baron's chest. Holding her close, he also tried to check her for injury. "Are you hurt?"

A paramedic came over. "Let's check her out over here." She motioned to the ambulance.

Mutely, Baron nodded but would not let Manda go. As the paramedic checked her out, Baron saw that Cass was being brought out on a stretcher. "Cass? Cassidy! What happened to her?" he asked the paramedic. He could see that her face was very pale.

"Overdose."

"No. No way. Absolutely not! She doesn't do drugs."

"They'll do a full workup at the hospital. Your little girl is fine but I would suggest bringing her in for a full work up too."

Baron looked over to where they had Ranger on the ground. "What the hell? Get off him!"

The paramedic looked over at the door to the house and nodded her head. "His wife shot and killed some guy from what I understand."

Baron was silent, then, "What? What guy?"

"Some guy named Anderson from what I understand. We have to go. Are you riding with us or bringing her on your own? We need to get the other patient to the hospital."

Baron stood up with Manda and fumbled for his phone. "Dad," his voice was brittle. "Come to the house now. Bring Priest."

A man in a suit walked up to him and flashed his badge. Baron could see that he was a detective.

"You treat your own this way?" he asked the detective through gritted teeth.

The detective looked over to where Ranger was being put in a patrol car. "Hey! What are you doing with him?"

"He was combative. Taking him in," the officer responded, shrugging. "He tried to stop us from taking his wife in."

The detective frowned. "That doesn't sound like him."

"Take it to your captain."

CHAPTER 29

"Mr. Murphy, can we go somewhere to talk? The kitchen has been cleared," the detective offered.

"What's your name, detective?" Baron asked him.

"Gustafson."

"Detective Gustafson. I have no idea what has happened here but something stinks. This smells like pig shit from where I am standing."

As they entered the kitchen, Manda's head was laying against Baron's shoulder. She had cried herself to sleep. Baron sat down, weary, and held her close. "Detective, if you wake my daughter right now, I will take you to hell myself."

"Mr. Murphy. Let's step back from all of this for a moment. Your tone is not appreciated and uncalled for."

"Is it? What has taken place here today? What I know is we buried my Mom today and then everything blew up at my house."

"Shit. I'm sorry to hear that."

Baron shook his head. "Explain what has happened here. Be clear. No bullshit."

Gustafson sat back and assessed Baron. "From what we have

pieced together, Brent Anderson was in the house. We don't know why. We found a young lady, unconscious, behind the desk in the office. Anderson was dead on the floor. He was shot three times. We found a .380 that we think was the weapon that killed him. Until ballistics are run, we can't be sure. We will run forensics on the syringe as well, to determine what was in it."

Baron sat silently. He had been assessing what he could of the house from where he sat. There was evidence of a scuffle. Part of the molding was gone from the corner heading to the hallway.

"I need to lay my daughter down." He didn't wait for a response. Getting up, he headed to her bedroom, taking notice of everything in there. Nothing seemed out of place. He hated leaving her in the crib, but he had to get back to the detective.

"Oh God, baby. What happened here?" Baron whispered to her, rubbing her back. Placing a blanket over her, he left the room, leaving the door open.

As he came to the kitchen, he saw that King was leaning against the counter. Priest was in the detective's face. He looked at his Dad, who simply shook his head.

"Where the fuck is my wife?" Priest yelled, bringing his fist down on the table in front of Gustafson.

"Mr. Murphy. You need to step back from me," Gustafson began.

"Mr. Murphy checked out, fucker. You are dealing with Priest now. People don't like him. He isn't a nice guy. Where are Josh and Claire? Speak now. I am out of patience and you have no backup."

"Your wife shot and killed a man."

"What? Motherfucker, that is crazy. She couldn't do that. Not a chance!" Priest shook his head in   disbelief.

"It was Brent Anderson," Baron told them.

Priest's head snapped to the side and King stood up straight.

"Her kidnapper? The man who tortured her? You arrested her

for that? Is that where Josh is now? Detective Wilkes to you," he sneered at Gustafson.

"They arrested him too after beating the shit out of him," Baron replied.

Priest roared.

"Listen," Gustafson said. "I am doing my best with what I have right now. I know Josh too. I know the history with your wife and Anderson. Between the suspected overdose and the homicide."

"It was not a fucking overdose!" Baron said through gritted teeth. "She was dosed. Still unconscious when they left. I have been patient, Detective, but I need to check on her. She only has us as her people here."

"Not till we are finished."

"Jesus. What else?" Baron snapped.

"You can speak to the club attorney," King told Gustafson.

"You are under no duress," Gustafson began.

"Doesn't matter. You are done here," King stated, eyes icy. "Both of you go check on your women. My granddaughter will be at the clubhouse with Dani and me. She will be safe along with Nate."

"So that's it?" Gustafson asked, perplexed.

"That's what I said," King said simply, leaving the room.

CHAPTER 30

Baron entered the hospital and asked for Cass's room number. His mind spinning with everything that happened, the biggest thing was how Anderson got into his house despite his and Bigs' security. There had been no alert and the person who had been assigned was missing. Baron suspected they had been hacked. But by who? His teeth grinded together so hard, he could hear it as he rode up in the elevator to the floor with Cass's room.

As he waited for the nurse to give him an update, he looked around the hall for exits and points of entry. She came back and told him Cass had been awake and had confirmed she was okay with visitors. Thanking her, Baron walked to her room. He saw that Otter was sitting outside the room. Giving him a chin lift he pushed the door open to her room. Baron was relieved to see Romeo sitting beside her bed. They hugged it out. Looking over, he saw that she was asleep again.

Seeing his concern, Romeo spoke up. "She'll be in and out for a while, until the drug is out of her."

"Do they know what it was?"

Romeo shook his head. "They'll run tests. Until the bloodwork comes back, it will be hard to say. A strong tranquilizer is my guess."

"Not an overdose. Could Anderson have done this to her?"

"Not an overdose. Doubtful she would choose to dose herself by sticking a needle in the back of her neck," Romeo said idly.

"Fuckers, the cops said she overdosed. They arrested Claire and Ranger."

"Yeah. I saw them take him in. Claire was already in the car. They used way too much force on him, though. It wasn't deserved. He is a big man, but if they had let him see her, he would have been fine, in my opinion."

"Something is wrong about all of this. We are out of our league. Priest has gone to the jail."

Romeo snorted and shook his head. "That a good idea?" he asked, squinting at Baron.

Baron shrugged. "Dad is getting in contact with the club attorney and I wasn't going to try to stop him. He was unhinged."

"Where are the kids?"

"Dad has them at the club. I think he may want to lock us down until we can assess what is happening."

"Jesus. We aren't this type of club where stuff like this happens, man. What is happening to us?"

"We're protecting our own." Baron looked at him and held his eye.

"Fair enough. I'm going to see if Otter wants a break. You want anything?"

"Nah. Thanks, though."

Romeo slapped his hand on his shoulder as he walked by and left the room.

***

Baron sat by Cass' bed, emotionally drained. He texted Pretty to check on Nate. Nate was playing video games, not a worry to be had. Baron was relieved beyond words. Rubbing his eyes, he looked over at Cass. Leaning over, he brushed her hair back.

"Baron?" she said, sleepily.

"Hey there."

"Am I still in the hospital?"

"For now, yeah."

"How did I get away from him?" she whispered.

"Doesn't matter right now. Just rest."

"Will you hold me? Please? I'm scared and I hate it," she hissed.

Baron got up and lay beside her. Wrapping his arms around her, he rested his head on hers. Guilt was eating at him.

"I'm so sorry, Cass!"

"What? Why?"

"I feel like this is my fault. Me and my fucked up life!"

"Stop that. Your life is blessed with family and friends."

"And you," he murmured.

Sometime later, Baron awoke with a crick in his neck. His arm was numb. He attempted to move and groaned.

"You alright?" he heard, making him look down.

"Yeah. You?"

"Better. Kind of. I feel like I am hungover."

"Oh no. Let me get the nurse," he said, attempting to get up.

"Baron. Stay. I'm okay. Really, I am."

Worry creased his brow. She reached up a finger to smooth the crease away.

"What are you thinking?" she asked him.

"How this could have ended," he groaned, leaning his head back against the bed.

"But it didn't. How did I end up here?"

"Claire."

"Oh. Where is she?"

"That's a long story. We'll talk later."

"No need to put it off. I don't have any pressing plans."

Sighing, Baron got up. Standing with his back to her, he placed his hands on his hips.

"Uh oh," she thought out loud.

Baron walked to the door and looked outside the room. Otter and Romeo both looked up at him and gave him a chin lift. Nodding, he shut the door.

Rubbing his face, he sat down. "Anderson got in the house?"

Cass nodded.

Baron swore and took her hand. "I am so sorry, Cass. That this fucker came into your life. I swear. He will never touch you again."

Squeezing his hand, she waited.

"From what we know, Claire came in and shot Anderson. Killed him," Baron said in a low voice.

Cass leaned toward him. "I never saw Claire there, Baron."

"Looks like Anderson injected you with something. A tranquilizer probably."

Cass gasped and touched the back of her neck. "He did!" she said urgently. "He said he would get a good price for me and Manda! Who would do that, Baron? What type of person does that?"

Baron stood up so fast that the chair he was sitting in crashed against the wall. Otter and Romeo rushed into the room with a nurse following closely.

"Sir, I will have to ask you to leave if you upset the patient!"

"We're leaving," Baron responded, looking at Cass. Nodding, she got out of the bed and headed for the bathroom to get dressed.

"Ma'am! You haven't been released!" the nurse said, following her.

"I'm leaving against doctor's orders and will sign any paperwork absolving the hospital and doctor of all responsibility.

I am going home. I need my kids," she said, looking to Baron.

A slow smile filled his face. "Yeah. You are."

CHAPTER 31

As they pulled into the club house lot, Cass looked at Baron.

"It's safer here. We have everyone here right now. Well, except for Claire."

"I can't believe they aren't saying where they took her! How can that be legal?" Cass said, outraged.

"It's bullshit. Right now though, I have to pick my battles. My concern is for you and the kids."

Cass looked at him. "Oh, Baron. You haven't even had time to grieve your mom."

A funny look came across his face, then he tapped his steering wheel.

Looking back at her, he placed both hands on her face, leaned over and brushed his lips across hers.

"I think I am falling for you, Cass."

"Baron, I have already for you. And your kids. You are mine!"

Kissing her harder, Baron swiped his tongue against her lips, loving her sweet taste. Moaning, she opened up to him. Their tongues lazily rubbed and their sighs mingled.

"Let's go inside," Baron said, against her lips.

Quietly, Cass followed him inside the building.

***

The clubhouse was somber. Baron looked left to right, trying to find his kids.

"There!" Cass pointed across the room.

Nate was sitting with King and Dani. Dani gave Manda her bottle. Nate was pushing food around on his plate. Priest also sat at the table. His face looked murderous. Baron had a bad feeling.

"Where's Ranger?" he asked Priest.

"In jail," he gritted out.

"They actually arrested him?" Baron asked, incredulous.

King looked up and pinched his nose. "We aren't sure what is going on. Reaper is doing his best to get information, confidentially. They won't tell us anything."

"What about the attorney?"

"Baron, right now, your family needs you. Look after them," King snapped. "Your son needs you."

Baron felt like he had been slapped, he felt a flush rise up his neck. He quickly pushed that aside and gathered Nate and Manda to head to his room. Once they were in his room, he would speak to Nate.

"You're not eating?" he asked gently.

"Not hungry," Nate mumbled, looking down at the floor.

Baron turned to look at King.

"He's having a tough time," King said, apology in his eyes.

"Mom?" Baron asked.

"That and his own Mom is gone."

Baron shut his eyes as his head fell forward. Shaking his head, he followed Nate and Cass, with Manda, up the stairs. Opening the door to his room, he found Nate sitting on the sofa. Sitting beside him, he put his arm around Nate's shoulders.

"You want to talk about it?" he asked Nate.

Nate shrugged and wiped at his eyes.

"It's okay to be sad. Losing family is sad. It isn't something we can prepare ourselves for, we should allow ourselves to feel. Keeping it bottle up isn't good for anyone."

"Are you sad?"

"Yeah. I'm sad. I will miss my Mom."

Baron wasn't prepared for the next question out of Nate's mouth.

"Do you miss my Mom?"

Baron blinked, realizing that how miserable Nate had been with Jade, she had still been his mother, a shitty one, but still.

Clearing his throat, he looked down at Nate. "Nate, honestly, I have a lot of anger when it comes to your Mom. She shouldn't have been the way…" *What do I say?* "I'm angry because she left both you and your sister, but at the same time, I loved your Mom. I wish I had been here more often. Maybe things would have been different. But I can't dwell on the past. I learn from it. I can only try to do better now and keep doing so in the future. I want to be the best Dad I can be for you and Manda."

"You are Dad," Nate said, sniffling.

"Thanks, Nate. I am going to do everything I can for you both."

Cass smiled at him from across the room. Baron gave her a weak smile. She frowned and turned her head away.

"You sleeping in here tonight, Nate?" Baron asked him.

"Yeah, I can pull out the sofa."

"Okay. Let me get Cass sorted and I will be back in okay?"

Nate nodded and began pulling the cushions off of the sofa bed.

Stepping out into the hallway, Baron motioned for Cass to follow. Closing the door, she followed Baron out to the hallway.

"Uh, I need to find a room for you or do you want to stay

with us?" he asked, rubbing the back of his neck, unsure.

"Baron, honestly, I think it best that we not sleep together. I am saving myself for marriage."

Baron sputtered. "Well...what...um, damn...I wasn't expecting that. You're a virgin?"

"I thought you knew..."

"Never occurred to me, honestly. I have been spending most of my time trying to not think about you like that," he said with a huffing laugh, his cheeks heating.

"You are so sweet," she said, kissing his cheek. "I want to get to know you better and take this slow. This would be a big step for you and for your kids. I meant what I said. I feel like all of you are mine. That doesn't mean we can be careless."

"I can respect that. Thank you, Cass. Thank you for everything you have done, especially not heading for the hills when all of this stuff started happening. Not anyone would have done that, you know?"

Cass nodded. "We have time. I want to spend it with all of you."

Baron looked down with a grin and then back up at her. "Let's find you that room."

EPILOGUE

Claire sat in the back of the patrol vehicle. After she saw the sign stating they were in the state of Georgia, she yelled at the men in the front of the vehicle.

"Where are you taking me?" She had asked before, but as with the previous attempts, there was no response.

Sometime later they pulled into a road that lead to a jail. Her heart rate kicked up again. The car stopped and she was jerked out of it and dragged into the jail. She was booked and searched. Her face flamed at the rough treatment. Her clothes were put into a bag and taken away. She sat there, nude, waiting to see what would happen next. A female guard came in and gave her a prison shirt and pants. She was also given rubber shoes.

"I want to call my lawyer," she told the guard, pulling on the clothes.

The guard nodded, turned Claire around and handcuffed her again.

"Where are you taking me?" Claire asked, hating how her voice shook.

The guard pushed her toward a door. They entered a long

hallway that lead to some jail cells, men were on one side and women on the other. As they walked through the jail cells, the inmates called to her. Her blood chilled.

"King don't have no power here, skank!" "They coming for you, he can't help you here!" "Priest should have left well enough alone and let them keep you!"

The guard opened a long jail cell and pushed her into it. Once the cuffs were off, the guard stepped back, closed the door and made sure it was locked. Claire turned and sat on the bench seat, ignoring the taunts that were sent her way.

The chatter and taunts suddenly stopped. The silence was almost as frightening.

Someone hissed, "He's coming for your now…"

Claire could hear someone whistling. The whistling came closer. Out of the corner of her eye she could see a tattooed hand run along the bars of her cell. Looking down, she saw cowboy boots with metal tips. The whistling stopped. Glancing up, she saw a man covered in tattoos, wearing rose colored glasses and a cowboy hat.

"Who does she belong to?" he asked the inmates.

"The Big Bad!"

"Where is she going to?"

"The Big Bad!"

She could hear crazy laughter after that. Someone began chanting, "Pope, Pope, Pope…" Soon all the inmates were chanting it. Claire covered her ears, the voices were so loud.

The man held up his hand and the chanting stopped. As quickly as the hand had gone up, it came down and reached through the cell bars, grabbing her by the hair. Hauling her toward him, he leaned down.

"You give those boys in South Carolina a message for me. You'll do that for me won't you, Claire? Pretty Claire. Hmm?"

Claire didn't dare move. The pain was so bad, she was afraid he was going to pull her hair out. Her eyes watered, but she refused to cry. Biting the inside of her cheek, she ignored the pain.

"You took something that belonged to the Big Bad, pretty, pretty Claire. That won't do. Oh no. Won't do at all. You take this message back to King, Priest, and Ranger. Oh yeah. Especially Ranger. He and I go way back. You tell him Pope sends his regards. You'll be seeing me soon again Claire, pretty Claire. Don't forget that, you hear?" he said, almost seductively.

She shuddered and slid away from him, huddling against the wall when he let go of her hair. She looked at him full on then. She would never forget the man's handsome face. It was terrifying.

ACKNOWLEDGEMENTS

Seeing as how this is only book 2 of the series, I really need to thank the readers who asked for it after reading Blind Love. You all have made the difference in me thinking this is okay for a hobby to, hey, someone else really likes what I am writing! Thank you!

Next, I thank my Betas, Tammy, Brittany, Nancy, and Megan. They set about the task and asked very good questions and gave encouragement that I needed after the tough year I have had. Yes, I know the steamy sex scenes were non - existent. Sorry. Straight up erotica next time. Swear it!

Finally, I thank Rhiannon and Virginia for their patience with me. Being a new writer is one thing but topping that off with the year that I have had…pfft. You two are saints!

Printed in Great Britain
by Amazon

77656415R00082